LIFE'S TWISTS

Carol Fike

Author's Tranquility Press
ATLANTA, GEORGIA

Copyright © 2024 by Carol Fike

All rights reserved. No part of this publication may be reproduced, distributed or transmitted in any form or by any means, including photocopying, recording, or other electronic or mechanical methods, without the prior written permission of the publisher, except in the case of brief quotations embodied in critical reviews and certain other noncommercial uses permitted by copyright law. For permission requests, write to the publisher, addressed "Attention: Permissions Coordinator," at the address below.

Carol Fike/Author's Tranquility Press
3900 N Commerce Dr. Suite 300 #1255
Atlanta, GA 30344, USA
www.authorstranquilitypress.com

Ordering Information:
Quantity sales. Special discounts are available on quantity purchases by corporations, associations, and others. For details, contact the "Special Sales Department" at the address above.

Life's Twists / Carol Fike
Hardback: 978-1-964362-58-8
Paperback: 978-1-964362-26-7
eBook: 978-1-964362-27-4

Chapter 1

It was a typical winter day in Manhattan. The taxi Page was riding in pulled up to the sidewalk just outside of her apartment. She gave the taxi driver a generous tip and then got out; snow fell as she climbed the stairs.

Her apartment was small in comparison to the house she had lived in as a child. She thought that it was a start, though, and the cheapest start around for the time being. Page had brought a few items along to decorate the apartment. She had bought pretty curtains for the living room, the kitchen, the bedroom, and the bathroom. She also had bought a clock and some decorations to fix up the apartment. In general, she stayed conservative with her money and didn't care to spend a lot—only what she needed to.

Page was establishing her own business called the Fashion Boutique, a medium-sized clothing store on the upper side of Manhattan three blocks from where she lived. Page had hired six girls to help her, who designed clothes at the factory where Page worked. Page decided what materials they used to make clothes. The girls made shirts, jeans, sweaters, dresses, skirts, blazers, jackets, and shoes, and at the store, they also sold purses and all kinds of jewelry.

All the girls worked hard, and the shop was quickly becoming a success. People from many different areas in the city were starting to shop at the Fashion Boutique. Women of all sizes and ages shopped in the boutique's petite, misses, plus, and junior departments. Much of what Page sold was unique and modern. The customers were very kind, and many were becoming regulars. Women told other women about the boutique. The store had a lot of sales, and some of them brought in a lot of extra business. But, overall, the store was becoming a huge success. All the hard work was all worth it in Page's eyes.

Page was young—only twenty-one—attractive, and very petite; she had a gorgeous figure. One of her attractive features was her long, blonde hair that she curled; it hung halfway down her back. She loved animals, but she couldn't have any where she lived. Page didn't have a lot, but at least she had enough to pay her bills. She figured with the extra income she was now making from the boutique, she would put some aside and put some into fashion so she could keep trying out new clothes for the business. For now, the store was all she had, and she gave it her all.

Page's days started early. Monday through Friday at six o'clock, she had some of the girls open up the store to take inventory early and mark down seasonal items. On the weekends, the boutique opened at seven, which gave the girls a break. On holidays, the store was closed; The Christmas, Thanksgiving, and Easter seasons were busy times, and Page had to hire more staff to maintain the business. The store was always busy in the summer months as well, from the end of March to the end of September.

The business was running smoothly; the current fashions were exquisite, involving fall colors and pretty prints. A lot of Page's designs became best sellers, and the store's popularity was increasing. Page had been considering adding on to the store. She knew that if she did, she would have twice the work to do, and she would have to hire more girls to help with the business. Page was having difficulty squeezing everything in to her busy lifestyle, and she didn't know if she wanted to complicate her life even more. Luckily, her youthfulness allowed her to do everything required of her, so, after being open for two years, she finally decided that it was time to add on, and she was fortunate to have the funds to do it. The store had a huge basement, and Page hired a crew of men to fix it up for the men's and children's sections, which she had thought about previously. The items they were designing for children and men were very nice. Page anticipated that they would be big sellers as well.

All was quiet that night as Page settled into bed. She slept very soundly after a hard day's work.

Chapter 2

The morning was young as Page awoke, like clockwork. She got up and made a cup of coffee, which she always had first thing in the morning. It woke her up and started her day off right. Page had a busy day at the boutique planned. When she got to the store, the girls were busy setting up different displays with the new articles of clothing from the shipment that had arrived at the store the day before.

A lot was going on, and business was booming. Quickly, fall, one of the store's busiest seasons, approached. Halloween was right around the corner, and the store was stocking costumes of all kinds for men, women, and children. People went out and about buying Halloween items. It was a time of year that people were very upbeat about, with haunted houses and barns and such in the area. Trees stood colorful and bright.

After Halloween ended, the boutique's overstock merchandise went on sale. The girls stayed busy getting the Halloween items marked down for sale. Thanksgiving was fast approaching, and they had new apparel arriving daily. Page planned on going on a vacation to Cancun around Thanksgiving, relying on the girls she had hired to take care of the store and keep it running. Page had a few close friends and was going to spend the holiday with them. She and four of her friends all pitched in to pay for the trip. Leaving for Cancun, they boarded the plane and all sat close together as they talked and shared time with one another. They had a wonderful time on the plane, and when they arrived in Cancun, the weather was fantastic. They spent ten days there. Time flew by, and before they knew it, it was time to take the flight back home.

When Page and her friends arrived back home, it was midnight in New York time. All was well, and Page arrived tanned, laid-back, and ready for work the next day. She didn't go to her store until later the next day. At the Fashion Boutique, everything seemed to be running smoothly. The girls had the store set up nicely and in order. This confirmed that Page had very responsible girls running the store. She knew she could rely on them while she was out of town. Now, some of the girls were also going to take their turns to go on vacations, some of them with their boyfriends. They all got vacation time as well as paid holidays. The boutique was doing quite a bit of business; sales were up. Page and the girls were considering a line of children's clothes for boys and girls of all ages. They figured they would have the new children's clothes by spring, probably by Easter. Easter would be a good time of year for the store and the swelling merchandise.

The girls who worked at the Fashion Boutique really liked their jobs, and Page treated them with respect. Some of the girls were older than Page, closer to thirty years old. One of Page's top-paid girls, Jessica, was married and had twin girls, who were turning one year old; they were the spitting image of their mother. Jessica had a lot of knowledge in the fashion world. She came up with ideas for the store quite frequently. Jessica; her husband, Josh; and their two girls, Eli and Ashlee, took a cruise in the Bahamas. They left early Saturday morning and stayed for two weeks. They had a lovely time. The weather was great, all that they expected it would be.

Page also had other girls whom she put a lot of faith and trust in. Brooke was a well-liked person. She was older—forty years old, but she looked as if she was in her early thirties—and her hair was very long, and she wore it in many different ways. She was a natural blonde and very pretty, to say the least. All the customers liked her and valued her opinion. A lot of new ideas for the boutique were Brooke's; many of the store's displays and ideas for selling clothes were hers. She really gave her job her all. She had a college degree in retail marketing and management. She was very intelligent and knowledgeable in many areas and did an excellent job. Brooke and her husband lived just outside of Manhattan. She had always wanted children, but she never could carry one to full term, perhaps because she worked too hard; Brooke always did as much as possible. She had been pregnant three times and hemorrhaged every time. The fetuses had always positioned themselves in her fallopian tubes. She lost two girls and one boy. One girl had been four months along, and another girl had been five months along. When she was seven months along, she lost her boy. These were very devastating times for Brooke and her husband. They were, however, considering adoption. She did want children, and she was willing to try anything. Brooke didn't know for sure if adoption was going to be an option, though.

Eventually, Brooke and her husband had their prayers answered by an ad in the newspaper, which said that a young woman had a baby girl that she couldn't support and she was going to give her up for adoption. The young girl was only sixteen. She wanted to keep the baby, but she wasn't married, and the father of the baby was a drug addict. She didn't have a place of her own either, or much income. Brooke felt bad for her. She talked to the young girl and told her she didn't quite know everything she was going through, but she would take very good care of her little girl. As Brooke and her husband fell asleep that night, they knew things were looking up.

Chapter 3

The next morning was the start to a very crisp December day, only two weeks until Christmas. The snow was starting to fall. Everything showed signs of the season; the streets were decorated with lights and holly, and Christmas decorations were strung above the street.

When Page awoke, she looked outside her bedroom window. Then she showered, had breakfast, and got ready to go to her store. When she arrived, all was going well. They had received a new shipment for the holiday season. People were starting to gather just outside the door. The store was opening soon, and the girls were busy taking inventory of the new arrivals. Some of the girls were putting the new clothes out for the customers to look through. Some customers had ordered special items for family, friends, and coworkers for Christmas, including jewelry, articles of clothing, and gifts of all kinds. The store and the atmosphere around it were bustling with people. The weather was cold, and people were all bundled up. The girls decorated the tree in the store window, and they were also stringing lights across the ceiling. All was looking very festive.

Page planned on going to her parents' ranch in Arizona for the Christmas season and the New Year. She was going to leave that Monday, one week before Christmas, and spend two full weeks with her family. She usually spent the holidays with her family; she put aside time just for that. Her parents, Patricia and John, had plenty of room for her in their beautiful home. Her mother was an excellent cook, and she kept an immaculate house.

Page had a big family, three sisters and four brothers. All of her sisters and brothers came home for the holidays. Some of them lived nearby, and some of them lived outside of Arizona. Two of Page's sisters were married and had children. One sister, Paula, had two girls, ages one and two, and another sister, Becky, had one three-year-old boy and a four-year-old boy. Her other sister, Jackie, who was twenty years old and in college, was dating a boy. The girls, all natural beauties, all resembled each other. Two of the sisters had really blonde hair, and the other one had black hair. Page's brothers all kind of looked alike also. They resembled their dad. They ranged from age six to age nineteen. They were all in school. One of the boys, David, was a freshman in college. All of Patricia and John's children were very intelligent.

Patricia enjoyed writing books. She had written children's books and had started writing novels. She had written one novel, and she had started writing her second one. She was an excellent writer. Her children's books were best sellers, and her first novel was currently being published. She hoped it would be successful as well. She was an exceptional wife, spouse, mother, and writer. She also helped out on the ranch when she could. She helped feed the cattle and the horses. She took excellent care of herself, and she didn't look anywhere near her age.

Page felt welcome at the ranch. It felt like home, as always. She and her family had a yearly tradition where each of them opened one small gift on Christmas Eve. The whole family looked forward to it. As Christmas passed and New Year's fast approached, Page realized it would soon be time for her to go back to New York. She didn't mind, though, because, after being away from her shop, she looked forward to making sure that everything there was done in a timely manner. She also knew that after Christmas and New Year's, there would be a lot of markdowns to make and the place would be busy. They always had good business after the holidays.

The new spring line was in focus. They were starting to get ready for Easter and spring in general. Easter would be in March that year. It would be arriving early.

As Page was getting ready to leave her parents' ranch a day after New Year's Day, she had many things to pack. She had had a wonderful time, as always. She would be flying out of Arizona the very next day and would arrive in New York that night. She planned on taking the weekend off and going back to the boutique on Monday morning. Page knew she would have a lot to catch up on.

When Page arrived at the boutique Monday morning, things appeared to be running smoothly. She talked to the girls, and they said that sales had been good during the holidays. The girls at the store informed her of everything that had happened when she was gone. The holidays were behind them, and things were getting back to normal. Sometimes Page wondered what normal was. They were getting some items ready for markdowns so that they could get the holiday inventory moving. The store was opening up, and people were coming into the store. Clearance items were selling fast. When the store had markdowns, the inventory seemed to move rapidly.

The next few months flew by, and Easter was near. They had a shipment of Easter clothes and accessories. Everything showed signs of Easter. People's years contained Easter lilies and other flowers. Everything was bright, sunny, and new. It seemed that all was going quite well, as far as the boutique was concerned. Page had been invited to go see her family in Arizona in one week. She had decided to drive this time. She never turned down an invitation, regardless of how busy things seemed to be. Besides, it was almost the only time when she saw her family. Page went to her parents' home. She arrived two days before Easter.

Page's parents had hired hands to run the ranch. They had six ranch hands to take care of their twenty horses. They had to run the horses, groom them, feed and water them several times a day, clean their stalls, and be there when they had shows and such. Page liked one of the guys, Blake Turner. She was attracted to him. He liked her as well. They were starting to talk to one another, and they went riding together several times. Blake thought he would ask her out a few times before she had to return home again. They really thought a lot of each other.

On Easter day, Blake and Page spent the day together at Page's parents' place. They went out on dates at a nearby restaurant called the Farmers Diner several times. The restaurant cooked homestyle food; Blake and Page enjoyed their food. It was their favorite restaurant in the area. It was in a pretty primitive area; there wasn't a lot around. One had to drive thirty miles to get to a grocery store.

The Easter holiday flew by all too quickly, and then it was time for Page to leave. Blake and Page stood, embracing each other, kissing, and holding on to one another. They hated to part. After Page climbed into bed that night, she dreamed about Blake, and Blake was at his ranch with his thoughts on Page. Who knew where they would go from there and where fate would take them.

Chapter 4

Monday morning, Page awoke early because she had a lot to do. She went to the boutique, where markdowns on Easter merchandise were being done. She thought about Blake and the time they had spent together. She had had a wonderful time and couldn't wait to see him again.

Her cell phone rang; it was Blake on the line. "How are you, sweetheart?" he asked.

She quickly answered and told him all about the boutique and her business. He told her about the ranch and how things were going there. He said they were preparing for a horse show. They were very busy grooming the horses and running them. They had them out on the track pulling a buggy. He told her that they were doing a good job. The horses had to be put through a lot of training to do this kind of work. Blake and Page told one another how much they missed each other, and then their conversation ended. Page and Blake missed each other. They longed to see one another again. They were quickly falling in love. It was just like love at first sight; neither one knew if they believed in that, but they knew how much they cared for each other.

Blake decided to fly to New York to see Page in two weeks. He wanted to surprise her for her birthday—to do something special for her. He bought her an expensive bracelet, and he planned on taking her out to dinner and a movie. He liked spoiling her in that way.

As Blake got off the airplane, he called Page. She was happy to hear his voice. They would meet each other that night, and he was going to take her out for pizza and to a Broadway play. She wore jeans, a cashmere sweater, and high-heeled shoes. The evening was kind of chilly, so the sweater felt good. She carried an expensive Italian leather handbag. Blake had on jeans and a sweater, and he looked very handsome. They were an attractive couple. Page's hair was put up in a neat bun. She always looked good, regardless of how she wore her hair. When Blake saw her, he remarked on how lovely she looked. He was proud of her, and he liked being in her company. She made him feel like a real man.

They held each other, arm in arm, as they talked, walking down the street. Everyone who saw them seemed to respect them and gave them second glances. They had a wonderful time that night. When they got back to Page's apartment, they had a bottle of Chardonnay and some snacks. They had one more night to spend together before Blake had to leave. Blake suggested they spend the night together by going to a nearby theater to see a movie. The movie was hilarious, to say the least, and they both felt as if they had never laughed so much. When the movie ended, Blake asked Page if she would like to find a hotel to spend the night at. She agreed that it would be a good idea and told him she would like that. There was a big screen TV, a huge bed, and a Jacuzzi tub in the room. They ordered room service and had sandwiches and other snacks and red wine. They were falling for each other very quickly.

Blake slowly undressed Page, and they made love. They filled up the Jacuzzi and sat in the warm water, talking and sharing their lives with one another. They seemed to have a lot in common. They got into bed and made passionate love throughout the rest of the night. They were not interested in sleeping because they knew their time together would fly by. Page laid her head on Blake's chest and talked, telling him how much she would miss him. Together, they shared everything possible. How great life was when they spent time with one another.

In the morning, they made love one more time before they each showered and had to go their separate ways again. The look in Page's eyes said it all. She looked sad at the thought of leaving Blake. Her huge blue eyes said everything, and as she looked at him, his eyes looked sad also. Each of them knew they wouldn't see each other for a while. It was all they could do to say good-bye to each other. Blake and Page stood kissing and clinging to one another. Blake had to leave Page at the terminal. It was like leaving a small child there. She looked so sad. Blake said he would call as soon as he got back to Arizona. It would be a full month before they could plan on seeing one another again.

As soon as Blake got off the plane in Phoenix, Arizona, he gave Page a call. On her end, she answered and was happy he had called but sad that he wasn't with her. She longed to see him again. They tried to sound happy, but in reality, they were both sad.

Blake and Page called each other daily for the next month. Blake was planning a special trip. They would fly to Paris and stay there for ten days from the end of June to the middle of July. Page had talked about wanting to go there, and Blake thought he would surprise her. She said that she wanted to get ideas for a new fall line for the boutique. She wanted special clothes—items that she knew would be big sellers. A new line of colors would be nice also. She got tired of the basic black and white.

The clothing items she was thinking about were new and not seen a lot. Special orders would have to be made for some of the items just in case they didn't sell. Page had in mind tunic sweaters that would work well with leggings or jeans, a new line of sweater dresses, designer jeans, tie-dye shirts, button-up shirts, sweater leggings, and hoodies of all kinds and sizes, as they seemed to be big sellers. She thought about tailor-made coats and dresses and a new line of handbags, shoes, and boots of all heights, as they worked well with a lot of the attire. They also wore quite well and were versatile in all kinds of weather. She also planned for a line of outerwear for children and all kinds of clothing for men as well. She knew some of the different items would go quickly and some styles just wouldn't appeal to customers. While they would get things that went well with everything, they would order more of certain items. That made business boom, and profits would go up. Things were going quite well as far as everything in Page's business was concerned.

The day was quickly coming to a close, and Page was tired as she climbed into bed that night. Her thoughts went to Blake as she dreamed of him and slept until morning.

Chapter 5

Blake and Page were preparing to go to Paris. Page was packing her suitcases. She was taking a lot of clothes. She had several pairs of jeans, very stylish dresses, tunics and leggings, sweaters, several pairs of shoes and boots, different kinds of shirts, skirts, a blazer, and intimate apparel. She felt as if she was overpacking, but she wanted to look terrific, and she wasn't sure what the weather would hold.

Blake was also getting ready for the trip, but he packed only what he thought was needed: a couple of sweaters, some pullover shirts, jeans, and a pair of better shoes and a blazer just in case the weather was chilly. He also took along some dress slacks and a versatile jacket for when he and Page went out. He wanted to look good and be at his best for Page.

The two of them were as excited as small children waiting for Santa Claus at Christmas. They couldn't wait to see each other. They also knew all too well that their days there would fly by all too quickly, and then it would be time for them to part again. They hated that thought, though, and tried not to dwell on it.

Blake called Page, and they talked endlessly about everything. They would meet at the airport. That way, they could fly to Paris together. When they met at the airport, they kissed and hugged one another and told each other how much they missed each other. When they boarded the plane, the airline stewardess greeted them and showed them to their seats. They were both happy and excited to be together. They talked on and on and shared their thoughts and feelings.

The stewardess told the people the usual things they needed to know for the flight. The plane was full of passengers, and on the other side of Page and Blake sat a young couple with two small children. There was a little girl, Page guessed around two years old, and she had a little brother, whom the mother and father were holding on to consecutively. They looked happy to be there, and they talked endlessly to each other and their children. Their daughter kept looking Page's way, and the little girl started talking to Page. Page asked her what her name was and introduced herself to the girl. Page found out that her name was Logan and that she was two and would be three in four months. Page thought she was very cute, to say the least.

After they started talking, the little girl opened up, and she talked and talked. Page and Blake had to laugh to themselves about how talkative she was. She was upbeat and expressive. The parents also were friendly and talkative. They told Blake and Page where they were from and what they did for a living. It turned out that they were both successful. The father's name was Keith, and he was a doctor, and the mother's name was Nicole, and she was her husband's assistant. They worked together at the same facility. The mother told them that they had been planning this trip for about two years and that they needed to get away for a while and relax. Page told the couple a little about her boutique, and to her surprise, they said they would have to look it up when they were in the area. Blake told them where he lived and what he did for a living also.

The two couples had a terrific time on the flight. They seemed to talk endlessly together; they were friends by the time the plane was ready to land. Blake, Page, Keith, Nicole, and the children liked each other, and they planned on doing something special together while they were there. As the plane was ready to land, the stewardess told the people what to do. The six friends told each other their good-byes and said they would be keeping in touch.

Blake and Page were finally in Paris and very happy to be there. Together, they walked arm in arm as they looked around and were amazed by what they saw. They wanted to see everything they could. Together, they felt like little children at a candy store. Everything looked new and exciting. Blake and Page were so happy to be in Paris that all their cares and concerns seemed to fade away. How sweet their lives were as they enjoyed each other's company. They saw the Eiffel Tower, and they went through numerous shops. They couldn't get enough of each other; their time together would fly by, but for now, they were living in the moment.

As the first day in Paris was coming quickly to a close, Blake asked Page where she wanted to dine. Page picked out a restaurant called the Cafe Diner. It was a very elegant restaurant, and the food there was excellent.

Page and Blake were renting an expensive townhouse to stay at while in Paris. They just wanted to eat, go make hot, passionate love, and explore each other's bodies for the entire night. When they finished eating, Page and Blake went to their townhouse. They barely made it to the door, as they were already kissing and holding on to each other. When they made it through the door, they started undressing each other. They were in bed before they knew it, engaging in lovemaking to the fullest extent. When finished, they lay spent, happy, and pleased to be there. They talked on and on, and then they made love again. Their bodies stayed entwined together; all night, through and through, they talked and made steamy, uncontrollable love to each other. It felt right to both of them. They just wanted each other so much.

In the morning, when Blake woke up, Page was standing in the nude, making him an omelet, bacon, and coffee. He couldn't contain himself as he looked at her. He put his hands all over her, and before they knew it, they were back in bed once again, making love. After they finished making love several times, they got in the shower together, still making love. When they were finished, they got dressed and went out to see what they could of Paris. Page wore a pair of slacks, a floral blouse, a blazer, and high-heeled shoes, and she had a stylish handbag that she had bought the day before at one of the Parisian shops. Blake had on jeans, a shirt, and an expensive leather vest. They looked so good together. They just seemed to tick, like a clock in motion. They looked so attractive and meant to be. How wonderful life was when they were out and about with one another. Even where they were, in Paris, people gave them extra attention. It felt right to both of them just being there with one another.

It was lunchtime when they left the house. Blake and Page picked out a small restaurant called the Bristol Cafe. When they went in, the hostess showed them the food bar and gave them their menus. Blake and Page decided to eat outdoors since the weather was fantastic. It was a warm, sunny day—not too hot, not too cold, but just about as comfortable as could be. They talked and reminisced about their lives and how much they cared for each other. They loved being in one another's company. The setting said romance, and romance was in the air and all around them. The two of them seemed closer than ever, and they could barely contain themselves. They wanted each other so badly they could feel it in their hearts, their minds, and their souls, to their very core. After finishing lunch, they went to a nearby museum, and they held on to each other as they walked through it. They were so close that they moved like one person, one body, one being in motion. How great life was when they were seeing and doing things together.

After Blake and Page left the museum, they kissed, hugged each other, held on to each other, and hurried back to the hotel. When inside, they started to undress each other almost instantly and climbed into bed. They spontaneously made love to each other. They couldn't contain themselves as they clung to one another after their passionate sex. Blake and Page just kissed and talked and held each other. They talked about everything from their childhood years to what they liked and disliked, what kinds of food were their favorites, their families, and even a little bit about getting married, which was very surprising, since they had only known each other for a short while. It was as if it was destined to be. Life was good, as far as they were concerned, when they were with each other.

After lovemaking, they fell asleep in each other's arms and slept until morning. In the morning, they made love, showered, got dressed, and called room service for breakfast. They had pancakes with syrup, sausage, and coffee. After they ate, they went to some different shops, and Blake left Page to shop endlessly until lunchtime. She bought two tunic sweaters and leggings to go with them. She also bought a couple of dresses and two blouses, a pair of stylish shoes, and jewelry to match the colors of her outfits.

When Page joined back up with Blake, they had a wonderful time. They had Italian food—lasagna—for lunch, with salads and rolls with butter, and raspberry tea, which was their favorite drink. The two of them had a lot of the same likes and dislikes. After eating, they decided to go to a nearby park and see everything they could there. It was all new to both of them; they felt like two small children at an amusement park, getting on and off their favorite rides and enjoying their favorite places. Neither of them wanted their time there to end. They wished they could just be together forever, without responsibilities. At the end of their busy day, they had steak tartare, baked potatoes, breadsticks, sweet tea, and blackberry cobbler for dessert. The food was delicious. At the end of the day, they walked back to their place hand in hand and began their lovemaking to the fullest extent. They were truly in love with each other.

They undressed each other and sat naked in the Jacuzzi while they talked endlessly. Blake looked lovingly into Page's eyes. He said everything he wanted to say to her as he sat with his arm around her shoulders. "I love you so much," he said, "and you mean the world to me. I've loved you since we met. You are the sweetest person I've ever known."

Page was looking into Blake's eyes also, and she told him the same—that he meant the world to her and she could never love anyone more than she loved him. She said she didn't want to live without him, and she was lonely without him.

"When we are apart," Blake said, "I think about you endlessly. I think fate and heaven and the good Lord above brought us together. I don't know what it is about you, but you are the only girl for me, and I thank God that I got to know you." Blake and Page were truly meant to be as they sat and explored every inch of each other's bodies. They knew all too well that their time together in Paris would soon fly by, and they wanted to get as much out of the time they had there as possible. How sweet life was when they were with each other. Everything was wonderful as they shared their time, thoughts, feelings, and emotions and their loving relationship.

After spending time in the Jacuzzi, they went to the king-sized bed, where they made love once more. They fell asleep in each other's arms, and they awoke in the morning in each other's arms and touching noses.

Neither of them wanted to get out of bed, but the day was new, and they wanted to see more of Paris. They showered, dressed, and ordered breakfast in the hotel room. After breakfast, they went out on the town.

The next few days seemed to fly by quickly. Page called Nicole, the friend she had met on the flight. They decided to meet at a little restaurant called the Paris Diner. Keith, Nicole, Logan, baby Luke, and Blake and Page all went out together. They talked and laughed at each other's jokes and had a very exciting time. They went to a nearby movie theater and saw an excellent movie called *The Last Flight*. At the end of the day, they told each other that they would get together and go to the swimming pool the next day.

It was midnight when Blake and Page got back to the hotel. They stood together, hugging and clinging to each other. They kissed and looked up at the stars. It was a warm night, and the stars were bright. Blake and Page stood for a long time. They had two more days in Paris left. One was to be spent with their new friends, and the other they thought would be spent alone at the hotel. For their last day, they wanted to be together as much as possible.

Once at the hotel, they went inside, undressed each other, climbed into bed, and made love until they couldn't contain themselves. Then they got into the Jacuzzi, held one another, and talked. Afterward, they got back into bed and made love over and over. They fell asleep and slept until morning, when they had breakfast and then met their friends at the pool and swam all day. They talked to Keith and Nicole and told one another that they would keep in touch. The day went by all too quickly, and in the evening, they decided on where they would have dinner. Then Blake, Page, Keith, and Nicole went back to their hotels to get ready.

When they got to the hotel, Blake and Page made love, showered together, had sex in the shower, and got dressed to go out. Page got all dressed up, wearing a blue sweater dress and high-heeled shoes. Blake had on a western shirt, a vest, and jeans and a pair of cowboy boots that he had brought along for special times out such as this.

They found a restaurant called the Honey Cafe Restaurant. When inside, Keith, Nicole, their two children, and Blake and Page were greeted by a hostess and seated. They were given menus, and they each chose the large salad bar, which had a little bit of everything on it. They ate and talked endlessly, having a wonderful time together. They all agreed that the food was very good. After they left the restaurant, they said that they would keep in touch.

Blake and Page decided to walk back to their hotel. They went back holding hands and talking. Once inside, they kissed and made love until they saw stars. Each time felt better than they could imagine. It felt right to both of them.

The next day when they woke up, they lay side by side, and they told each other that they were sad because this was their last day in Paris. They were going to miss each other badly. They cherished their last day together. Neither of them wanted to leave the room. They just wanted to cling to one another, make love, talk, and enjoy each other's company. The day flew by, as they figured it would, and as much as they hated to, they showered, got dressed, and went to dinner. They had a good time, but a time of sadness in a sense because they knew their time together was slipping away. They took advantage of the night by staying up and making love, kissing, and talking.

The night flew by, and in the morning, Blake phoned room service and ordered breakfast for two. They had eggs sunny-side up, bagels with cream cheese, sausage, and coffee to drink. They started to pack, as they had to leave in three hours. Page was sad, and Blake felt the same way because they had to go their separate ways. Blake told Page that they would get together very soon, if he could help it.

They got dressed and took a cab to the airport. They were kind of quiet for a change as they boarded the plane. They held hands while on the flight. Gestures seemed to talk for themselves, and the looks on Blake's and Page's faces were very sad.

When the plane landed, Blake and Page said their good-byes. "I'll call you tonight," Blake told Page. They kissed each other; it seemed as though it would be ages until they saw each other again.

Chapter 6

Looking back to the day before, Blake found it hard to believe that he and Page had been sharing a bed in Paris. Meanwhile, Page's alarm clock was going off, and she tossed and turned in bed, not wanting to face the day yet. Her thoughts were still on Blake and the time they spent in the City of Love. She had exactly one hour to get ready for work. She climbed out of bed, showered, ate breakfast, and got dressed. With fifteen minutes to get to work, she was out the door haling a taxicab. When she got to her store, the girls were preparing for the day. Brooke was unlocking the doors to let the customers come in. The boutique seemed as busy as usual. Page asked how everything had gone while she was away. The girls gave her a rundown of everything she needed to know. It all sounded good. The girls asked Page how her vacation had gone and what Paris was like. Page said that Paris was a very exciting place and that they had had a wonderful time. She also said that the time there flew by all too quickly and vacations are never long enough.

Days and weeks went by, and Blake and Page phoned one another daily. Page got a phone call around eight o'clock one night; it was Blake on the line. They talked for about an hour. They couldn't wait to see each other.

Page had been feeling sick to her stomach. She suspected it was the flu or something, and she continued to feel upset and under the weather. She never thought about missing her period. She hadn't told Blake about how she had felt lately. She knew he was always busy and didn't want to upset him in any way about herself. She decided one day to call Dr. Gibson. She went in as scheduled, and he took some tests. The following day, Dr. Gibson's office called and told her that they needed to see her. She just thought they were going to tell her it was something that was going around. She went, and Dr. Gibson told her that her stomach problems were due to being pregnant.

"How many months along am I?" she asked.

"Well," he told her, "You are about eight weeks pregnant."

"I guess Blake and I did get a little bit careless while we were vacationing in Paris," she said. She went on for another full month and didn't tell Blake. She didn't know how to break the news to him.

One night, Blake called around two o'clock in the morning. Page answered, sounding sleepy. "It's your dad," Blake answered. "He had a massive heart attack around midnight, and he had to be life-flighted to a nearby hospital."

Page was hysterical. She could hardly believe what she was hearing. "How can this be?" she asked. She was very upset and concerned at the same time.

"He was working way too hard. He had overexerted himself, and it was an ungodly hot Arizona day. The heat and his age were both against him. They have him under sedation, and he's hooked up to all kinds of monitors and tubes. He's holding his own as of right now. Your mother is with him, but he isn't alert enough to know she is there. She keeps talking to him. The doctors and staff told her that this would help to keep him stable and alive. She cried every time she saw a straight line on his monitor. She would get hysterical and call the nurses to come in and check on him."

It was an extremely difficult time for her entire family. On her end of the line, she said that she would have to pack and get the first flight out that she could. There seemed to be so much that she had to tell Blake. She couldn't wait to be near him and feel his skin on hers—to be next to him trying to make light of everything that was happening. She felt as if they had to be together all the time now, since everything else seemed to be going wrong. How could she tell him everything? She knew that they loved each other after their romantic encounters in Paris; she felt it in her heart. She knew Blake would understand what she was feeling. *How could he not understand?* she asked herself.

Page showered, got dressed, and packed three bags because she knew she would need them. She planned on staying for a month or more. She wanted to make certain that her dad felt better before she decided to return home. If he managed to pull through—and she could only hope that fate would step in and her dad would survive—all would be well again. All she could think about now was her dad, the baby growing inside her, Blake, and what her mother must be going through. All these thoughts were spinning around in her head. She knew she had a lot of decisions to make.

She was ready to go. She skipped breakfast, which she knew, in her condition, wasn't in her best interest. She hailed a taxicab, and as she got in, she said, "Take me to the nearest airport."

The flight was kind of dull, as she had no one to talk to and she wanted to keep everything that was going on to herself anyway. She really wasn't in a talkative mood, with all that was taking place. In flight, she never thought about the boutique, given all the things that were happening.

Finally, the plane landed, and it was time to deboard. When Page walked into the hospital, she wondered how everything was going. "How are you holding up?" Page asked her mother.

"Not very good," her mother answered. They stood hugging each other with tears in their eyes.

Page had a lot on her plate, with everything that was going on. *If only my mom knew,* Page told herself. Page looked at her dad and could only hope that he would survive. She thought that things weren't looking very good. There wasn't much the family could do but be there for him. The doctor told them that was as important as anything else he could possibly think of.

Blake called Page to tell her that he was on his way. When he arrived, Blake and Page embraced each other. The way they looked into each other's eyes said it all to Page's mother. She could tell instantly that there was a spark between them. However, she didn't know anything about their lovemaking in Paris or that Page was carrying Blake's child. Page wasn't showing yet, so she didn't have any explaining to do as far as Blake and her mother were concerned. She wanted to say something to Blake, but she kept it all in. She wanted to be alone with him anyway when she broke the news to him.

They were all concerned about her dad and her mother, considering what they were going through. They all stayed in the hotel room during the night. Page's mother kept calling on the doctors as she felt was needed, and she could hardly gain her composure after seeing a straight line on the monitor. She cried out each time something seemed to be wrong. The doctors did all they could every time. They stayed busy all night.

In the morning, Page's dad was still just holding on; he stayed this way for about two weeks. After the second week, he started making some improvements. When Page's mom talked to him, he started making movements in response to her. He was becoming alert, which was a good sign. It made the family feel better to see that he was coming around.

John would go into assisted living after being in the hospital. The doctors thought that he would have a complete recovery, which sounded good after what he had gone through, but there would always be the possibility of a setback. With John getting out of the hospital, Page would return home, after being with her family for more than two months. Page had a lot to do when she returned home. When she returned home, she called the boutique and inquired as to how things were there. The girls said that it was kind of a slow time, but things would be picking up again in a few months. Everything was starting to look up again, aside from the fact that Page was about four months pregnant.

Page climbed into bed that night thinking back on the last two months, her dad, her mom, Blake, the baby, and herself. She wondered what Blake would think about their child, and she hoped that they would be together again very soon.

Chapter 7

In the morning, Page woke up in New York, and Blake woke up in Arizona. Things were back to normal, whatever normal felt like. Page had breakfast, showered, and got dressed. She put on a pair of her favorite leggings and a maroon sweater. The sweater hung loose around her middle so no one could see her baby bulge. She had on a pair of knee-high boots, and she carried an expensive leather handbag and wore jewelry to go with her outfit. She brushed her blonde mane of hair over her shoulders. Everything about her said *sexy, elegant,* and *beautiful,* and there wasn't a man alive who knew her who didn't feel this way about her. Page was a one-in-a-million girl, and not only that, she had morals. Everything about her seemed to stand out: the way she looked, the way she carried herself, her outlook on life. She always wore a smile for the world to see her pleasant attitude. You would never think anything in her world could go wrong. She did have ups and downs, though. She was just excellent at not letting things show. She was also a true believer in the Lord, and she attended church on a regular basis.

Page had a doctor's appointment with Dr. Gordon. She was almost six months along. Dr. Gordon told her that the baby was healthy and growing very well. He could have told her the sex of the baby now, but she said that she wanted it to be a surprise, and besides that, Blake had no idea that she was even pregnant with his child. It was fast becoming a reality that she would have to tell him soon. She only hoped that he could accept the fact that it was his child and that marriage was possibly in their future. That would probably be the best option in her condition, but she thought to herself that she didn't want to be a burden on anyone, especially Blake. He was, however, the father of this child, and she was going to break the news to him really soon. She knew she would have to because they were planning on getting together again. She was driving to Arizona to see him and visit her parents in exactly three weeks. Her dad was feeling a little under the weather these days, or at least that was what her mother kept saying. He had good and not-so-good days, and Page wanted to see him. She would be showing, and besides that, it was time to let the family know about Blake and their child.

She was calling and texting Blake on a regular basis, or he would call and text her. Page also kept up with the boutique; she went to the store on a daily basis to make sure things were running smoothly and that the girls were running sales in a timely manner. Page's employees were responsible. They had things at the boutique running right on time. Page was lucky in that sense. That was one thing that she didn't have to worry about. This was good, since she had her family to be concerned about. Blake and their baby were on her mind all the time. In a way, she was ready to tell Blake and get it all out in the open. *It's time,* she thought to herself.

The next day, Page was getting packed to leave for Arizona. She was taking several suitcases. She packed a lot of loose shirts, leggings, and some bigger dresses. She also was taking along sweaters for chilly Arizona nights, because it was turning into fall. In the fall, Arizona did have some colder nights. She was staying for quite a while this time; she figured around two months or more. She only had three months of pregnancy left, and she was thinking about staying until the baby was born. She was going to talk it over with Blake and see what he thought. Page only hoped that he would agree that she should have the baby in Arizona. Maybe she wouldn't leave, Page was thinking to herself. Maybe he would want to get married so that they could be together, share the birth of their child, and be a family. *Mrs. Page Turner,* she thought to herself. It did sound very good to her, and she wanted to be married more and more. If only he knew how she felt. Words couldn't describe how she felt; the true reality of it all was that she felt alone, lonely without Blake. She decided that whatever happened, it would be for the best. She believed that you have to put your best foot forward and do the best you possibly can, and she certainly lived up to that.

Page was packed and ready to leave in exactly six hours. She was wearing a pair of gray stretchy leggings, a gray loose, variegated tunic sweater, and her favorite knee-high boots. She had her hair up in a bun, and she had expensive earrings and a watch on in colors to match her outfit. She looked gorgeous, as usual. She was very young looking, and she wore just enough makeup to make her look like a movie star.

This time, Page drove toward Arizona in the car she had purchased at a little nearby car lot. She bought it used for the small price of four thousand dollars. It was a far cry from being brand new, but it ran well, and she had always managed to get where she was going; to her, this was all that mattered. She figured that she would drive for eight hours and then find a place to stay and arrive in Arizona the next day. She wasn't in a big hurry this time, only seeking to see Blake and her family, so she thought she would take her time. She decided not to push it too far. It was around ten o'clock when Page found a hotel room and pulled over to spend the night. She called Blake to let him know where she was, and then she freshened up and went to find something to eat.

Page wound up eating at a small diner; she had salad, pasta, and breadsticks and raspberry tea to drink. Then she went back to her room and fell asleep until six in the morning, got up and showered, put on her makeup, and got dressed in a black pair of stretch leggings and a loose, button-up sweater. It was purple and well worn, but that was just the way it was made. She put on her knee-high boots, grabbed her purse and luggage, and headed toward the car. She drove the rest of the way, stopping as needed. Finally, she was in Arizona. She had about seventy-five miles to go. She could barely wait as she drove along. She was so happy to be getting close to Blake that she could almost feel him next to her. She only hoped that he was very happy about their unborn child and that he wouldn't be upset.

Page saw Blake in the distance. He was busy feeding the horses. Turning, he saw Page and immediately walked over to her. He kissed her as she got out of the car, and they embraced each other. Blake picked her up off her feet and twirled her around. He could feel that her stomach was bigger, and he knew instantly why it was a little bigger. He put his hands on her stomach and said to her, "Are you expecting?"

She answered, "Yes, I am. I'm six months along."

"I am so happy," he told her. "We're going to have a baby!"

She felt excited and relieved at the same time. "I was thinking that I'd stay here in Arizona till the baby is born," she told him.

"Sounds good to me," Blake told her. He felt like the luckiest man alive, to have a girl like Page, who was having his child. Who knew, at this point, where fate would take them.

Chapter 8

Page and Blake woke up in the same bed the next morning. How good it felt to them both. Page and Blake made love that morning and showered together, and then they got dressed. They really weren't in any hurry. They had all day to do what needed to be done. How sweet life seemed to them both. They were finally together, and maybe for good this time.

Page started looking in the yellow pages for a gynecologist. She found one and set up an appointment. Blake said he would go with her. This time, Page and Blake would find out the sex of the baby. *It's time,* Page thought to herself, and they were together now. The doctor she saw, Dr. Bradford, set up an appointment for the next week. During the appointment, Page and Blake thought that the doctor had an excellent disposition.

Dr. Bradford checked her and told her that the baby was growing very well and that it was healthy. Page laughed, saying that the other doctor she had been seeing had said that as well.

"Would you please reveal the sex of this baby?" Page asked.

The doctor looked at the monitor and answered, "It's a girl." Page and Blake were very happy.

"I guess we'll have to start discussing girls' names," they told each other. They both felt blessed, and Blake mentioned possibly getting married before the baby was born. Page was so happy at the thought of it; she could hardly believe it. It not only sounded good to hear him say those words now, but it seemed that they should get married, not only for their sake but the baby's also.

LIFE'S TWISTS

Page and Blake broke the news of their baby girl to Page's mother the next day. She was happy but also felt it would be best that they get married.

Blake took Page out to a nearby restaurant for dinner and a movie. After the movie, he popped the question. "Page, will you marry me?"

"Oh my," she said. "Yes, I would be more than happy to."

He, in turn, handed her a beautiful engagement ring. It looked nice and felt good on her finger. They kissed, embraced, and talked about setting a date. They both agreed that an outdoor wedding at her family's ranch would be a good idea. They planned on keeping the wedding simple. Page would get a gown, and Blake would wear a white blazer. They would plan on around two hundred guests. Blake's best friend would be his best man, and Page's sisters and the girls who worked for Page would be the maids of honor and the bridesmaids. Page had a three-year-old niece who would be the flower girl and a four-year-old nephew who would be the ring bearer.

Blake and Page agreed that they would have to get the invitations sent out within a week because they wanted to get married before their baby was born—December 18, one week before Christmas. Page had eleven weeks to go. She started sending out the invitations immediately. She got a lot of replies saying that people would be there. Some said that they had already made other plans. She had expected it to be that way. Time flew by quickly. Everyone was overworked, and with the wedding so close, all Page and Blake could think about was the baby and how in love they were, hoping and praying that everything would go well, as far as the wedding was concerned.

Everything was going along as expected. The wedding was only two weeks away, and Page only had a little more than a month to go before the baby would be born. She felt as big as a whale, although she didn't look it. She had been a small person to start with. To Blake, she just looked like she was expecting, and he was so happy that they were together and so much in love, that they were getting married, and that she would soon have his child.

He was a lucky man, and he knew it.

Chapter 9

With only one more week to go until the wedding, Page felt overwhelmed. She felt like being alone with Blake; she wanted to go somewhere they could be alone together. She wanted to be with Blake like when they spent ten days and ten nights in Paris. That seemed like a dream now, and a new life was inside her because of it. *How sweet that was,* she thought to herself. They seemed to have loved each other from the start. It seemed like a miracle come true.

Page regularly phoned the boutique to talk to the girls and see how things were going there. They were so happy for her. She mentioned to them that she may want to stay with Blake. Right now, as long as Blake agreed, the girls agreed that this was for the best. Page said that whatever Blake and she decided to do, she was going to try to keep her business. She thought that even though it was in New York and she was in Arizona, keeping the boutique in her name was still worth the effort. She considered starting a business in Arizona or maybe just selling the boutique. She was trying to make so many different decisions, and everything seemed to be happening at once. Blake was planning on a honeymoon in Paris for a couple of weeks, but he was kind of waiting until their baby girl was born. That way, he figured that they would both be able to enjoy the trip.

The day of the wedding turned out to be both happy and exciting. Blake got dressed in his white tux and tie. He had cowboy boots on—fancy ones —and a Cartier watch, one that Page had given to him for his birthday. He looked handsome and sexy, to say the least. He could hardly wait to see his lovely bride. Page was getting ready as well. Her sisters and friends helped her. With her dress and makeup on, she looked pretty and sexy, and she could hardly wait to see her new husband.

The day was absolutely gorgeous, with ninety-degree temperatures and sunshine to light the sky. The setting was lovely, with flowers on each guest's seat. Everyone chatted and got along very well. Music played in the background. Guests were told that it was time to take a seat. The best man and the groomsmen lined up and waited for the bride, the maids of honor, and the bridesmaids to come down the aisle. The setting was kind of tense, as most weddings are, and besides that, Page was with Blake's child, and that made for mixed emotions.

As the love song played, the maids of honor appeared in the aisle, and everyone in attendance stood up. The maids of honor had on pink dresses with blue flowers. The bridesmaids followed and were dressed much the same. They all wore strands of pink and blue flowers in their hair, and they carried pretty bouquets of pink and blue flowers, ribbons, and baby's breath. They all looked very attractive. Then "Here Comes the Bride" came on, and Page appeared. She stood on the arm of her father, and they walked down the aisle together. Blake looked at her, and he thought to himself that he was a lucky man. She was a beautiful bride. She was showing a little, but the gown she had picked hid most of the baby bulge. Together, Blake and Page joined hands in matrimony. They went through the marital rituals, and they placed rings on each other's fingers. They kissed, and then they faced the people as the new Mr. and Mrs. Turner. Everyone stood in line to hug them and talk to them. They took a number of pictures, and then they all met at the mess hall.

Everyone had a choice of chicken, steak, or prime rib. They could also have either baked potatoes or French fries, and everyone had a salad with the choice of dressing. After they finished eating, everyone danced with the bride and groom, and they talked, and almost everyone of age had some sort of drink. At one point, Blake and Page cut the cake and fed a piece to each other. Music continued playing, and the reception lasted half the night.

Blake told Page about his plans to take her to Paris again. She was so happy and excited to hear this. He told her that they could go after she had their daughter, and she thought that sounded like a good idea. She had about a month to go, and she was ready for it to be over. She told

Blake that she felt really big. All he could say was "I love you anyway, and besides, you are very pretty just the way you are. I love you, Page, and I love our daughter."

Blake and Page spent the night of their wedding in a nearby hotel room.

They barely slept; all they could talk about was what they would do in Paris, their wedding, and their new baby girl. They made love gently because Blake didn't want to bring on premature labor.

Blake and Page went house-hunting the next day. Blake wanted to do everything he could for his family. They looked at several and saw some they were interested in and others that they thought weren't what they wanted. They saw one in particular that was absolutely gorgeous. It had high ceilings in the living room, the dining room, and the kitchen. It had a rustic look, with a roomy kitchen that had everything possible in it. It had four bedrooms upstairs and two and a half baths. One bathroom had a shower, and the other two had roomy tubes. One room downstairs had a big Jacuzzi in it, and there was a big swimming pool outside. Page fell in love with it. She loved the whole house, and so did Blake. The best part was that it was affordable. It had 160 acres and a big horse stable. It was what they had both wanted and dreamed of. The main bedroom had some feminine features. It had a big four-poster bed with a lacy cover over the top. Throughout, the house was colored in pastels. It made Page feel at home.

They both agreed that they wanted the house, so they went to the bank and put a down payment on it and financed the rest. It cost $125,000. They put a down payment of $25,000 down on it. They worked out a reasonable payment schedule at the bank, one they could afford. Then Page told Blake that she had that much in the boutique, and at that, she thought about selling it, the circumstances being what they were. Maybe it would be best. She really didn't want the hassle of traveling back and forth, and she had a new addition to consider. It was another chapter in their book that was fast becoming a reality, and as they made love that night, Page knew that selling her business would be for the best.

Chapter 10

In the morning, when Blake and Page woke up, they made love, showered, and got dressed. They had breakfast, and Page planned on going back to New York because she had finally decided to sell the boutique for what it was worth. Besides, it would help Blake and her out in the long run. This way, they could pay for their new house and property. She knew that she could get that much out of it and maybe some extra. She hoped the girls whom she had hired would continue working there and that it wouldn't affect their jobs. She had a lot to think about and a lot of decisions to make. Blake had a lot of work to do also. They had a horse show scheduled to take place in one week. He was going to be busy grooming the horses and running them.

Page was packing to fly back to New York. Everything she packed was loose fitting. She only had three weeks of pregnancy to go. Blake teased her: "Don't have the baby in New York, or I'll have to fly out to be with you there."

She was feeling bigger than ever and couldn't wait to get it over with, but she told Blake, "I don't want to have the baby till I'm back with you." She kissed and hugged Blake and headed for her car. She left for the airport at noon. She would stay in New York for one week. When she got to the airport, she went through customs. She already felt lonely without Blake. After boarding the plane and taking her seat, Page was quiet on the flight. She didn't have anyone to talk to. She arrived in New York late in the day. She still had her apartment, so she spent the night there. The next day, she got up, took a shower, and got dressed. Then she ate and went to the boutique. When she got there, she hugged the girls. Some of them had just gotten back also, after being in her wedding. Page told them the news: that she had decided to sell the boutique for what it was worth. The girls had mixed emotions; they all said that they would miss her.

She replied, "Well, even though I won't own the store, I'll still be back periodically to be with you girls."

Page stayed for the week, just as she had planned to do. She called Blake on a regular basis and texted him often. She went to many real estate agents to find the best deal she could get for selling her business. She finally got an offer for $150,000, and she decided to accept it. It would pay off the house she and Blake had just purchased and leave an extra $50,000. She thought that she would put that money into a new business in Arizona.

She had a western store in mind, with various western clothes for men, women, and children, as well as cowboy boots, boots for women and children, and western outerwear. For women, she thought about skirts and dresses in many styles and sizes, western shirts and jeans, and jackets, shawls, ponchos, sweaters, and intimate apparel and pajamas. Page was fashionable indeed, and besides that, she knew what she wanted, and she was a very determined person. She would succeed in one way or another, and she had her mind set on that. She had made good money on the boutique, and she knew that she would do just as well in Arizona with a western store. She was thinking about calling it the Western Shop, and she had a good feeling about it already. She knew of a building that was already vacant close to the house she and Blake had just purchased. If there was one thing that was true about Page, it was that she would do anything to get on top of things and she would come out a winner every time. There wasn't anyone who could stop her once she had her mind made up.

Page had been in New York for a full week, and she was packing to fly back the next day. She went to bed early and got a good night's sleep. She got up early, and all she could think about was that she would be home with Blake soon. She got to the airport and boarded the plane. She sat by a young girl, Carrie, who introduced herself and said she was from Arizona also. Page said it was a small world, and the two girls talked and laughed. They got along really well. They exchanged phone numbers and addresses and said that they would try to keep in touch. As the plane got off the runway, Page kind of gasped, and Carrie asked her if she was okay.

Page answered, "I'm not sure. It's the baby. I'm having contractions." She told Carrie that she only had about two weeks of pregnancy to go.

"Hold on to my hand," Carrie told her. "I'll try to give you as much support as possible." Carrie kept telling her to hang in there and they would be landing soon—hopefully, before Page gave birth. "What are you going to name the baby?" she asked.

"I'm not sure yet. Blake and I haven't decided on a name. It's a girl, and I've been so busy, I just haven't taken the time to think about it. I'll have to decide soon." Page gasped again. This time was more intense than the last. "I wish I was at home with Blake," Page replied. "He would know what to do."

Carrie told the airline stewardess what was happening. The stewardess asked Page if she needed anything, and she said that if they had to, they would make an emergency landing.

"I wish Blake knew what I was going through right now," Page said. "I would call him if I could. Maybe I'll name the baby Taylor." "Take deep breaths," Carrie kept saying.

"I'm glad I have a good friend like you, Carrie, to help me," Page said.

"Just keep taking deep breaths, and we'll get you home soon."

"The contractions are starting to get closer and closer together," Page told her. She looked very uncomfortable. The stewardess told the airplane pilot to land at the next runway. She told him about Page, and he said that they would have to make an emergency landing.

About fifteen minutes before they would land, the look on Page's face spelled pain. As soon as they landed, Page called Blake and explained everything to him. She told him where she was—the area, the hospital, and all she could.

"I love you very much," Blake told Page.

"I love you as well," Page told Blake. They were about three hundred miles apart. Blake started packing as soon as he got off the phone. Once he was packed, he headed toward the airport and took the first flight out. While on the plane, all he could think about was keeping Page as comfortable as possible and hoping and praying that she would be all right. She told him that she was at the Arizona Regional Hospital, the western one; there were Arizona Regional West and Arizona Regional East. He hoped that she would be able to wait until he was with her to have their daughter.

Blake was in flight for about two hours. Then he got off the plane, hailed a taxicab, and told the driver where to go. When he got to the hospital, he looked around to see if he could see his wife. He went to the front desk and asked about Page, and they explained to him where she was. He went to her right away and bent down and kissed her gently on the lips. Anyone who saw them saw true love. Blake gently wrapped his hands around her and hugged her. "Hang in there, babe," he told her. "It'll all be over soon."

All Page could think about was that she was so happy to be with Blake. She told him that she had picked out the name Taylor Elizabeth Turner. He smiled and told her that he liked the name. Page was going to the delivery room. Being wheeled in, she looked scared, excited, and happy all at the same time. She would have more responsibility when her daughter was born, and Blake would as well. Blake held her, rubbed her shoulders, and tried to keep her as comfortable as he possibly could.

The gynecologist kept checking Page's vaginal area and told her that she was dilated ten centimeters. She was getting ready to bear down, and the doctor, who was named Dr. Baker, kept reassuring Page and Blake that the birth was going well. Blake kept rubbing Page's forehead; he was a concerned husband and soon-to-be dad. "Keep taking nice, deep breaths," the doctor told Page.

The baby's head appeared, and Dr. Baker told Page to push. She let out a scream. It was painful, to say the least, but it was a loving kind of pain, and Page was truly in love with Blake. When the whole head was out, Page bore down, and out came the baby's body. The doctor cut the umbilical cord and brought the baby back to Page. As she held the baby, Blake believed that he couldn't be happier. He was a very proud papa. That night, as Page went to sleep, she felt happy that everything had turned out for the best.

Chapter 11

They left Page to sleep until morning. They bottle-fed the baby that first night. When Page woke up that morning, the hospital staff had breakfast waiting for her. "Boy," she said, "did I sleep that long? I must have been tired."

"Labor usually does that to women," the nurses told Page.

Page called Blake to talk to him and see when he was planning on coming back to the hospital. He had gotten up early at five o'clock. He had already fed the horses and cleaned their stalls. He was having breakfast when Page called. He took a shower and got dressed. Then he drove to the hospital. They told him when he got there that his wife and new baby were doing well. They said that she could go home with him today, after being there for two days.

They discharged mother and baby with instructions to see the doctor where they lived for any problems that might be of concern and to receive follow-up care.

Blake pushed Page and their new daughter into the elevator by wheelchair, with Page holding their daughter. She felt good to finally be going home, where they would be a family. The nursery was all set up and ready for Taylor Elizabeth. Page got Taylor's middle name, "Elizabeth," from her mother, whose name was Patricia Elizabeth.

Once they were home, Page told Blake about her idea to start up a western-wear clothing store. She said that she had fifty thousand dollars, which would be enough to open the new store. She told him about the vacant building she had in mind. He thought that Page was very intelligent and the most determined person he knew, and he thanked God that he got to know her. He did, however, wish that she would try to spend more quality time with him and Taylor. She stayed home with Taylor as much as possible for four months, but she was always telling Blake that she would like to be back to work as a full-time person again. She said that work made her feel better about life, and it made her feel good to bring in her share of the money.

Blake, however, wanted to be the breadwinner in the family. He didn't know how to convince her that he would take care of things as far as working outside the home and the money situation was concerned. He knew that there was no telling Page that anyway. She would do more of her share, regardless, and if this made her happy, then so be it. Blake felt as if he would have been just as satisfied had she wanted to stay home and take care of Taylor, cook, and clean. He didn't know how she did everything that she did, and he was absolutely blessed by the way she did everything and still took excellent care of herself and him. *How did I find someone like her?* he often asked himself.

Taylor was five months old already, and Christmas was just two months away. Thanksgiving was only one month away. Blake and Page were spending the holidays at Page's parents' house, as usual. Blake suggested going on their honeymoon before Thanksgiving. Page agreed, and they packed that Friday and took Taylor to Page's mother so she could watch her.

"Are we going to have as much fun this time around?" Page asked Blake.

"I hope so," Blake said, "but do you want another baby this soon?"

Page only laughed and said, "If it is meant to be, I'll have another baby." It was fun making babies, and she loved Blake. If they had another child, it would give Taylor someone to play with, and it would also ensure that she wouldn't be an only child. She didn't want to stop with one child, anyway. She was so in love, and she loved making children with Blake. Page was open minded and mature. She thought that whatever would be would be. It was her time again, so she could become pregnant. This time, she wanted it to be the case, but she didn't tell Blake. She felt good about having another baby now, after the first one. She thought that she knew what to expect.

This time, she packed three suitcases full of stuff. She had jeans and T-shirts for warm days. She also had sweaters for chilly days and nights, dresses and boots, and high-heeled shoes for when she wore dresses. She took a sweater jacket and a longer jacket to wear with her dresses. Blake packed much the same as the last time. He didn't overpack or underpack. As they packed and got ready, Blake longed for Page. He felt the need to be pleasured. He played with her bottom and her breasts, and she wanted him just as much. They made love first in bed and then again in the shower. "You feel so good inside me," she said. He smiled at the comment, and it only made him want her that much more. When they were almost out of the shower, they both decided to have sex again.

"We better quit this," Blake said, laughing, "or else we'll never catch our flight." At that, they finished making love and got dressed. Page looked lovely; she had on jeans, a tunic top, and high-heeled boots that came up to her knees, and she carried a pink-and-gray leather handbag. She had on a long jacket that she had purchased in Paris the last time they were there. Blake looked sexy as well. He had on jeans, a pair of cowboy boots, a shirt, and a blazer.

They had some lunch, and they packed their car and headed for the airport. Once there, they went through the regular customs, and they boarded the airplane. This time, they sat toward the back of the plane. As they sat there, they talked endlessly, and Blake put his arm around his wife and told her how much he loved her. They sat there kissing and hugging, and they both wanted each other so much and could hardly wait until they got to the hotel room. Just looking at the two of them, one could see how much they cared for each other. This time, no one sat by them like the last time, with Nicole and Keith.

The plane landed in Paris as scheduled. Blake and Page felt like kids again. Something about Paris made people feel that way. Blake and Page checked in as soon as they got off the plane. They went to the room first thing, and they both had the same thing on their minds.

They decided to have a bottle of fine wine first to get their sexual desired started. As they sat on the sofa talking, laughing, hugging, kissing, and embracing one another, they started to undress each other. They made love on the sofa until they were spent. They both put their full effort into making love. Blake and Page not only made love, but they wanted each other to feel true love inside and out. After making love on the couch, Blake picked Page up and carried her back to the bedroom, where they made love again and again until they fell asleep in each other's arms and slept until the next day.

Then, when they woke up, they made love again, and they got up to take a shower together and make love in the shower two times. Then they got dressed to go out. Page picked out a dress that looked so good to Blake that he felt as if he wanted her again. She wore tights, a sweater over the dress, and knee-high boots, and she carried a red leather handbag. She looked stunning and very sweet and sexy. Blake wore jeans, a pair of brown cowboy boots, and a western shirt. He looked handsome, sexy, and stunning himself. They walked out of the room together, and they held each other as they walked down the sidewalk. They stopped at a coffee shop to have coffee, and then they had eggs, toast, and bacon for breakfast. Endlessly, they talked about everything, from Taylor, to Page's new western shop and Blake's work, to how much they loved each other. Blake and Page stopped at all the shops they saw, and Page picked out a new pair of shoes, a dress, two tunic tops, two pairs of designer leggings, and some new earrings, socks, and panties and bras.

Then they had lunch at a nearby cafe. Blake ordered steak tartare, and Page ordered chicken over biscuits; they each had a salad and light wine. They really enjoyed being together in Paris. The only thing wrong was that time was really flying by. That night, Blake took Page to a Thanksgiving play and to a skating rink, where the two of them skated. It was nearly midnight when the two of them went back to their room. On the way back, they stopped at a sandwich shop, and each of them picked out a sandwich of their choice. Page had to admit that Blake always tried to do fun activities.

They went to bed after watching TV and making love endlessly.

Page whispered, "What if I get pregnant again?" into Blake's ear.

"If it is meant to be," Blake said, "and if it's what you want, then it is just fine with me." Blake's reply made Page happy. They didn't go to sleep until the wee hours of the night. They weren't on a schedule, and they were enjoying themselves to the fullest. When they awoke in the morning and got up, they both felt stiff and sore from skating the night before. "I guess we're younger at heart than we are and our bodies can't take everything they used to be able to do," Blake told Page, and then they both laughed.

Page made Blake breakfast. She cooked eggs, bacon, toast, and oatmeal and made coffee, and he had orange juice. He ate a lot for breakfast. He believed that breakfast was the most important meal of the day. His mother taught him this when he was a child, and it stuck with him in his adult life. *He was raised with good morals,* Page thought to herself.

Blake thought that Page was not only sexy standing there making him breakfast in the nude, but also an excellent cook and a wonderful housekeeper. She took great care of him, Taylor, herself, and her business. He was a very lucky man. He didn't know how she could do all that she did. He often thought to himself that he couldn't do all that she did, or do it as well as she managed to. She truly was his better half, as the older generation would say.

Their days in Paris were quickly flying by. They had been on their trip for six days, and they only had four days to go. Blake and Page went out sightseeing, which they enjoyed, as they knew they would. There was so much to see and so little time in which to see it. For that evening, Blake had going to see a movie and then going out to dinner in mind. They had seen quite a lot of scenery that day, and they would move on in just a few hours. They went back to their room and made love, got into the shower, and had sex again and again. Then they got out and got dressed for dinner. Page wore a pair of leggings, a tunic sweater, and knee-high boots. She had her hair up in a bun; to Blake, she truly was the sexiest woman he had ever seen. She thought Blake was the sexiest man that she had ever seen, dressed in jeans, boots, and a blazer. They walked together down the sidewalk to the movie theater.

The movie was romantic. They both enjoyed the movie, and after it was over, they went to an elegant restaurant for dinner. They both ordered steak, a baked potato, and salad, and they had wine to drink. They stayed there, drinking wine and talking. They didn't realize how late it was getting. Both of them felt good, and when they decided to go back to the room, they undressed and made passionate love. Then Blake took Page into his arms and held her until they wanted more of each other. They made love over and over until they fell asleep and slept until morning in each other's arms.

The days went by, and it was just about time to go home. It did cross Page's mind that she may have gotten pregnant. It was just a woman's intuition. She just felt that way—why, she didn't know. She did hope that she was pregnant because she wanted someone for Taylor to play with. Page thought that being an only child would make for a dull life for Taylor. They packed their suitcases and took a shower the next day. They were leaving to go home at one o'clock.

They ordered room service for lunch, and they agreed on having just a sandwich, a salad, and a light wine. They had mixed emotions. Neither of them wanted to leave, but they did want to get back to Taylor. They had called Page's mother several times during their time in Paris to hear about how Taylor was doing, and while talking to Page's mother, they learned that Page's father had taken another turn for the worst. Page was in tears as she heard the bad news.

As they boarded the airplane, Blake and Page were filled with different thoughts of everything, from what they had done in Paris, to Page's father and how her mother had sounded on the phone. It was sad; all Page could think about as she got off the plane was that her father might not make it.

That night, as Page fell asleep at home, she thought about her parents.

Chapter 12

In the morning, after Page woke up, she searched for Blake, but he was already up, and he had already been out to the stable and fed the horses and cleaned their stalls. It was getting later in the day. Page and Blake went to her mother's house. They did not receive good news about her father. He had had a heart attack two days before, and this time was worse than the last time. They had managed to get him to the hospital, but it was looking very glum. He wasn't looking alert this time, but her mother did say that he had asked about Page. He had asked where Page and Blake were and why they were not at the hospital with him. Page's mother tried to explain the situation to him, but she couldn't get him to understand. He seemed very confused. Patricia even said that he had told her he didn't realize where he was this time. He was delirious.

That night, as Patricia got ready for bed, she received the dreaded phone call. It was the hospital on the line; they said that her husband had just passed away in his sleep. She got frenzied and started crying. "How can this be?" she asked. Patricia called all of her children and told them the awful news.

When she told Page, all she could hear was crying. Page sounded hysterical beyond belief. She said, "Why?" and took the news very badly.

The following day, funeral arrangements were being made by the family. They all had a lot to consider. John had only been fifty-six years old. That made Patricia fifty-two. They were so young. "How could this happen?" was all Patricia said over and over again. It seemed to have happened all too quickly, and now, Patricia was alone and lonely.

A lot of people attended John's funeral. It was a very sad day for the immediate family. The children were going to miss their dad, and Patricia was going to miss her husband. "What will I do without him?"

she asked herself. It would be difficult for Patricia to live without John. She cried a lot when she was in the shower or before she went to bed, and at times, she was alone.

A month and a half went by, and Page's thought that she was pregnant dawned on her again after missing her monthly. She made a doctor's appointment with Dr. Bently. He said that he would see her in two weeks. After seeing her, the doctor said that she tested positive; she was pregnant. She told Blake; he was very happy, and he said that he would like them to have a boy this time.

"I would like to have a boy this time too," Page told Blake. They agreed, however, that another girl would be just as nice. Page told Blake that she wanted four children altogether.

Blake smiled and said, "We'll see what we can do, Mrs. Turner."

About a month went by, and things were already gearing up for the holidays. "Where did the time go?" Page asked herself. It seemed to go by a little bit faster every year.

Page had a doctor appointment's that day. Blake went with her. Page had an ultrasound, and the doctor revealed that she was going to have twins this time. He said, "It looks like one of each."

Page and Blake were very happy with the news. Blake hugged his wife and told her that he was a very lucky man and that he was very glad to have someone like her. They both felt blessed and thankful for their children and for each other this Thanksgiving season. It was, after all, just around the corner.

The holidays were especially hard for Patricia. She felt lonely during these times. She had a hard time getting by, and she tried not to tear up in front of her children and grandchildren. It took its toll on the whole family in the long run.

This year, Page did the holiday cooking. She made the turkey, the stuffing, and most of the trimmings. Every one of her sisters took on a covered dish. Patricia missed John, and the kids all missed their dad. This Thanksgiving, there was a completely different set of emotions in the Turner household. John's passing was devastating. The family ate and said all that they were thankful for. They all had something to be thankful for, and even Patricia thought of something. She said that she was thankful for all her children and grandchildren. She also said that being with them was enough to give thanks for. She was happy that they were together, and she hoped for many more years together as a family.

Patricia was thankful for all the things she had, from her house and her vehicle, to being at Page's that year, to Page making her a grandmother again. This time, she was giving her double the fun, and one of each. It was like a blessing in itself. She knew in her heart that no matter how bad you think things are, someone else has it worse and is struggling more than you are. She told herself that; now, if she could just rationalize it. So be it; she told herself that she would try to make the best of it. She missed her husband and knew in her heart of hearts that she always would. She thought to herself that it was completely useless to pity herself; she knew that it would get her nowhere fast. She often told herself the old adage that it didn't pay to complain, because no one could help you anyway.

The family talked endlessly at the dinnertime feast. Page's sisters, her mother, and herself were going to go shopping together the next day. They figured that they would start their Christmas shopping early.

Page, her mother, and all her sisters got up, showered, and got dressed. They were all going to leave plenty early so they could spend the day together. Page had on a pair of her favorite blue jeans and a light pink tunic sweater. She also had on her favorite red leather boots. Page's mother was also dressed in jeans and a red tunic sweater. She had on a pair of blue boots. Patricia's other daughters were dressed much the same way. They were all going to an outlet mall. When they got there, it was hustling and bustling with people. There was a huge decorated Christmas tree at the center of the stores. Christmas music was playing, and people seemed full of the holiday spirit. People greeted other people, and everyone was friendly and outgoing and seemed extra nice. It was plain to see that people were in the mood to celebrate the season. Page, her sisters, and her mother all had a wonderful time; they shopped and shopped until they all decided where to eat.

All the women decided to eat at the food court. They ate rather light. They figured that they would stop at a steakhouse on their way home. They had bought a lot of stuff between the five of them. All talking, laughing, and telling each other jokes, the women shared a lot between themselves. There was truly nothing like the holiday season to bring out the best in people.

The women shopped till they dropped, as the saying goes. They truly didn't want the day to end. Patricia seemed more at ease than she had since John had passed away. This season truly had gotten everyone in the mood for giving. Page bought a pink, garment-washed hoodie. She also purchased two sweaters, a rose leather purse, a pair of red leather boots, and a sweater shawl in tan angora. She bought a new sweater with a hat and a scarf to match, and she also bought a poncho, which she fell in love with at first sight. She also bought a couple of pairs of earrings.

Patricia also went overboard. She bought the stores out, or at least it felt that way. She bought two tunics; a party dress, which she got at a good deal; two sweaters; some shoes to go with the party dress; and a blue leather purse. Like her daughter, Page, Patricia also bought some new accessories. She bought earrings and a necklace, a shawl, and some pajamas.

The rest of Patricia's daughters had bought many items as well. Some of the many things they purchased were for their children. Patricia had the same thing in mind and purchased several gifts for her grandchildren, along with many small items, like socks, undies, hats, mittens, scarves, and a few choice toys, which were bargains. Patricia purchased the boys' toys at a nearby toy store. The store had everything imaginable, as far as toys were concerned. She bought them a remote-control helicopter and a remote control big-wheel truck. The women stopped at the Long Horn Steakhouse on their way home. They all had a wonderful time.

When they got home, they all went their separate ways. Page and Blake made love that night, and they lay in each other's arms until morning.

Chapter 13

In the morning, Page and Blake woke up and made love, first in bed and then in the shower, and then they got dressed. Page made an omelet and coffee for Blake. He loved her cooking and the way she looked, dressed in a sweater dress, a pair of leggings, and high boots. He teased her endlessly and said he loved her over and over. She was in love with him also, but she was already pregnant and didn't need sex as badly as he seemed to need it.

Christmas was just around the corner, and Blake and Page were going to get a tree and decorate it. They planned on stringing lights and putting up various other decorations. That day, Blake was also getting special items for Page. He was taking the day off, and he decided to fulfill it that way. He had a couple of items in mind: a diamond bracelet, an expensive watch, and a brand-new red sports car.

Page also had a couple of items for Blake in mind. She wanted to get him a new diamond watch and a new sport coat. Page purchased other various items for Blake and her nieces and nephews. She also got items for her mother and herself. Page was into Mexican jewelry; she purchased a poncho that looked Mexican and a coat with an Aztec pattern, which also looked Mexican or western. She looked stylish.

Christmas was spent at Page's mother's house, but there was a void where Page's father would have been. He was sadly missed by all the family. Patricia tried to stay upbeat, but people could sense her loss and the emptiness inside of her. She still talked about John. At Christmas dinner, Patricia was unusually quiet. The girls all seemed cheerful, and they tried to bring the holiday spirit and the reason for Christmas to the table. They tried to cheer Patricia up, and it seemed to work temporarily, but she would go on being sad after the holidays.

After dinner, they all gathered around the tree to open their gifts. It was exciting. They received many gifts, and the children were all excited and upbeat. They all spent Christmas day together and stayed at Patricia's that night.

Chapter 14

After they went back to their home the next day, Blake and Page celebrated the rest of their Christmas gift giving. Blake gave Page her biggest gift, the sports car, before they went back to Page's mother's place. Page hugged Blake and told him how much she loved him. Blake told her how much he loved her also, and he told her all he really wanted for Christmas was her. Then they left Taylor at Page's mother's house so they could spend their weekend alone together.

Back at home, they started undressing each other on the couch, first in front of the fireplace, and then they went to their bedroom. Page had nothing on but a big red bow. Blake told her that she was the best present he had ever received. She laughed at his statement. She said, "You are the best Christmas present ever!" They made love until they couldn't get enough of each other. After making love, they fell asleep in one another's arms.

Blake and Page planned their New Year's celebration. They weren't quite sure yet what they wanted to do. They went out to dinner and then to a nightclub, and Page drank a little bit, but she told herself that she had to be careful not to overdrink. Blake, however, kept drinking. He got carried away and lost it completely. He started acting as if he wanted other women, and this was the first time Page saw him acting this way. She couldn't believe what she was seeing. He scarred their relationship with his actions that night.

Page left the nightclub that night with tears in her eyes. "How could Blake have acted so stupidly?" she asked herself. It was over, Page felt. There was nothing left in their marriage, as far as true love was concerned. *How could he stoop so low?* was all Page could say to herself. This all seemed wrong beyond belief. *I guess,* she thought, *true love—or what I thought was true love—can't last forever.*

Blake came home completely drunk the next day at five o'clock in the morning. He slept until one o'clock on New Year's Day. When he did get up, he smelled like a brewery. He tried patching things up with Page, but she merely told him that he was the one who had screwed up. She wouldn't give him the time of day, let alone talk to him. She felt that she didn't owe him anything. She could hardly believe that he could have let a thing like that happen. "How could he?" she asked herself.

Life seemed funny that way. It was all so stupid now, the way her life was turning out. Then she thought to herself that she must have been blind. "How in the world did this happen?" was all she could ask herself. She had one daughter and one of each on the way. *I guess that means absolutely nothing,* she thought. Blake had taken advantage of her, so she would leave him. She was going to pay dearly now, and he was going to have sex with any slut he wanted to. Page was truly ready to file for divorce. *One day, I felt as if I was on top of the world, and within minutes, it all fell apart,* she told herself over and over again.

When she confronted Blake with her decision the next day, he said to her, "Are you sure this is what you want?"

She merely looked him in the eye and said, "Why did you do this to me?"

He looked her in the eye as well and told her, "I was only talking to two girls, and you took it the wrong way."

"What was I supposed to do?" she asked him. "This was uncalled for, Blake," she said.

"Yes, and you can be sure it will never happen again," he told her.

She fell for him again after a week or so of thinking about the situation. She thought to herself that he truly was a loving husband and he did go out of his way to give her pretty things. At her age, she really didn't want to be alone without someone in her life. She thought that maybe she should give in to him again, but the question on her mind would always be with her now: Was her relationship about love or lust? She wasn't experiencing a full feeling of true love. When they did make love again, Blake was extra loving. He reassured her that nothing like this would ever happen again, or at least this was his reply.

Page only had a little more than three months of pregnancy to go, and she was wishing that it would soon be over. She was taking it easy and spending time with Taylor. Page knew that after the twins were born, Taylor might demand attention.

Page had a lot on her mind, with the twins on the way, and she was also thinking about her new business. She wanted to think about fixing it up and getting it opened up. The next day, she called several contractors for estimates. She got several different prices, from ten thousand dollars to twenty thousand dollars, and she decided on the lower estimate. She hired C and J Contracting to do the job. She heard that they were very efficient and that they would get the job done as quickly as possible. Page figured that, after having the twins, she would spend her time with them, and then she would start placing orders for her store.

Page had a lot of things for the store in mind. She was going to add a line of western jewelry for women. She decided on lots of beaded earrings in all colors and lots of western bracelets, watches, purses, and many boots for men, women, and children. She also planned on carrying unique items with different patterns, such as horses and Aztec designs. She loved colors, and different items caught her eye. She figured that people with a flare for fashion would have the same tastes. Page also had thoughts of creating her own line of clothing. She thought she would need more funds to do this, though, and she would also have to hire a bigger staff. Therefore, she decided to just do what she had to do to open the western store.

The day flew by all too quickly, and at the end of the day, Blake asked Page what she would like to do. She answered, "I would like to go somewhere for dinner." They went to a diner just down the street. Blake had steak and a baked potato, and Page had chicken and a baked potato. They both had salad and a light wine. At the end of the day, they were talking and laughing, and the trouble they had before seemed to be all but forgotten. Life was good, and as they went to bed that night, they made love over and over again. They fell asleep in each other's arms.

Chapter 15

The days went by rapidly, and the time for Page to have the twins was nearing. One morning, she got up and startled Blake out of his sleep. He woke up, reached for Page, and found her in a puddle of water. Her water must have just broken. She was having labor pains. Blake got out of bed concerned for his wife and called 911. They got on the line and told him to keep Page as comfortable as possible. The woman on the phone said that the ambulance would get to the house as soon as possible. She said that her name was Laura, and she asked what theirs were. Blake reassured Page that the ambulance was coming, and he did as he was told until it got there.

"Where do you live?" Laura asked Blake. As Blake talked to Laura, Page let out a sharp gasp of pain. Blake rubbed Page's shoulders while he stayed on the line to 911. "Hang in there, babe," Blake told Page. "You're doing a good job." Blake looked into Page's eyes, and as he did, he could tell that she was in a lot of pain. He reassured her that he would give her as much help as he could. "I love you more and more every time we go through times like this, Page," Blake said. "You don't need to talk; only listen and stay calm, if possible, until we get you help." Again, Page gasped and had another surge of pain.

It took the ambulance driver and crew a little more than half an hour to arrive. When they got there, Blake said to Laura, "They're here now. Thank you for all your help."

Laura told Blake that she was glad to help and she was happy for the family. "I'm glad that she did well," Laura said. The ambulance crew hurried, got Page onto the stretcher, and put her into the ambulance. "I'll follow you, babe," Blake said. "I love you, and hang in there." "I love you too," Page replied between labor pains.

LIFE'S TWISTS

They arrived at the hospital within an hour. The nurses and staff quickly got Page into hospital attire, and the doctor checked her to see how far she was dilated. He said that everything was moving along nicely. Page gave birth within an hour. With Page bearing down, the first baby's head appeared. As the doctor situated the baby, it came out, and the doctor exclaimed, "It's a girl!" Then Page bore down again, and the doctor exclaimed, "It's a boy!" Everyone was ecstatic, and Blake was more in love with Page than ever. He felt like a lucky man.

The nurses wrapped both babies up in blankets and gave them to Page and Blake. "We'll have to decide what to name the babies," Page said. Both parents felt blessed at that moment.

Blake bent over, gently kissed his wife, and told her, "You did a wonderful job, and I'm proud of you."

"Thank you so much," Page lovingly told Blake. The atmosphere spelled love, as far as everyone was concerned. Blake got on the phone and called his parents and Page's mother. They were all very happy to hear the news.

Blake went to Page's mother's house, got Taylor, and took her to the hospital. When she saw her mother, Taylor was concerned for Page. Taylor said to her, "Are you all right, Mommy?"

"Oh, yes, honey, I am. Do you want to see your new sister and brother?" "I do, Mommy," Taylor said. Taylor seemed happy to see them.

As they were all there together, Page's mother walked in and went over to hug her daughter. "Hello, Page!" she exclaimed. "How are you?" "Oh, I'm doing good. How are you, Mom?" Page asked.

"I'm pretty good!" her mother answered in reply.

Then, within half an hour's time, Blake's parents walked in and asked how they were all doing. Then they went to see the twins, just outside Page's room. Blake went with them. The three of them talked, and then Blake's mom went in to see Page.

The next day, Page decided on names for both babies: Jason and Kimberly. She was kind of stumped on middle names, but then she decided on Kimberly Sue and Jason Darious. Blake agreed that he liked both names.

After being in the hospital for three days, Page and the babies were told by the doctor that they could go home and be a family. The nursery was all set up for both the babies. For the first couple of months, the babies kept Page awake quite a bit. The days flew by rapidly, with the family getting used to the twins. Taylor was a bit demanding, since she realized that she wasn't getting all the attention anymore.

After about six months, the babies were sleeping through the night. They were good babies, and both parents were happy about that. Page started getting more and more ready to get her western shop opened up; she placed orders for a new spring line. Ideas flowed within her. She was truly an amazing woman, with a good head on her shoulders, and Blake didn't know how she did it all. All he knew was how much he adored her.

Blake and Page went to bed that night and made out three times before they went to sleep in one another's arms. The next morning, when they woke up, they were still entwined, and they made love once more before showering and getting the new day started.

Page prepared Blake and Taylor their breakfast, as usual. She made eggs, toast, bacon, and oatmeal. She enjoyed making breakfast, and like Blake, she felt that it was the most important meal of the day. As they ate, they planned their day. Page fed the twins after having her breakfast, and they all went on their way.

Page thought to herself that she was going to start buying miscellaneous items for the shop. She wanted to keep busy, and she always felt better about everything when she did just that.

The day was over before it had started; at least it seemed that way. Blake and Page made love several times, and then they finally lay spent in each other's arms, and they fell asleep until morning.

Chapter 16

Blake got up early the next day at five o'clock in the morning. He got dressed and then went outside to clean the horse stalls and feed and water the horses.

Page was sitting at the table reading a book when Blake walked inside. "Where have you been so early in the morning?" she asked.

"I've been busy with the horses," he answered in reply. Page had made pancakes, sausage, and coffee. "Breakfast smells very good!" Blake told her.

The babies started crying in the next room. Page went in to check on them. She bathed them, dressed them, and got them some food. They were both big eaters; they were really growing. Page took excellent care of her family. She took extra good care of herself and of Blake, and he knew it and respected her because of it.

"What's on our agenda for the day?" Blake asked Page.

"I'm going to work on my store," Page said. "I'm going to have it open as soon as possible. I'll start ordering items of all different kinds. I'm thinking of a name for my clothing line," Page said. "I think I'm going to call it Start Western Wear, and all the men's, women's, and children's lines will have the same name."

"That sounds very good," Blake said in reply. "I think I'm going to invest in a beach house in Miami, Florida," Blake said. "It would give us another home away from home—somewhere it would be warm in the winter months after the holidays."

"Yeah, that does sound like a good investment," Page said. "How much do you think that would cost us?" Page asked.

"I'm kind of thinking around one hundred thousand," Blake replied.

"Oh, is that all?" Page laughed. The phone rang, and when Page picked it up, it was her mother.

"Hi! How are you doing?" Patricia asked.

"I'm doing fine, Mom. How have you been?"

"Oh, I'm not doing too bad," Patricia told Page.

"It's good to hear from you, Mom!" Page exclaimed.

"Yes, and it's good to hear your voice," Patricia said to her daughter.

"How are those grandchildren of mine all doing?"

"They're doing just fine, Mom. What's new in your world?" Page asked her mom.

"Oh, I have a new beau," said Patricia. "His name is Mark Hamlin. We went out to dinner, and we went to see a good movie afterward called *Snowbound*. It was very suspenseful, and we both enjoyed it. We're going out again this Friday."

"That sounds exciting. I'm happy for you, Mom!" Page said.

"He's been married before, and he has three children—two girls, ages sixteen and fourteen, and one boy, who is ten years old," Patricia told Page. "Mark is fifty-six years old, and he is a doctor. He used to do operations, but now, he just sees patients in his office. He enjoys some sports, and he likes to vacation. He has been to a lot of different places, the way he describes it. He's very handsome. He has black hair, and he dresses very casually. He owns two different houses; one is in Florida, and one is here in Arizona."

"Blake and I are going to invest in a beach home in Florida," Page told her mom.

"Oh, that would be nice," Patricia said.

"Yeah, it sounds nice, but it will be very expensive," Page said.

"Well, I guess I better let you go and get on with whatever the day brings," Patricia said.

"Bye, Mom," Page said. "I'll talk to you again soon."

"Yes, and the same here," Patricia said. They kept in touch often, as many mothers and daughters do.

The day flew by quickly, and as Page and Blake got ready for bed, they made love. Who knew what tomorrow would bring.

Chapter 17

Mark called Patricia early the next morning. "Why don't we pack and go away for a few days?" he asked her.

"Yeah," she said, "that sounds good to me."

"We could spend a couple of nights in a motel room," Mark said. "Besides, I would like to get to know you better."

They were moving rather fast, Patricia thought, although she did have feelings for him and she did have an emptiness where John once had been.

She was in love with Mark, and she did want him as much as he seemed to want her, and at her age, she thought, there was no harm in it. After all, both of them had children from their previous marriages. The only difference was that her husband, John, was gone for good, and his ex-wife, Kelly, was still alive, and he had only been divorced for a short period of time. Mark talked about Kelly as if she had expected the moon and she had wanted her cake and to eat it too. He had caught her in bed with his best friend, and he had filed for a divorce a few months later. As Patricia saw it, it was over between Mark and Kelly, and he was a completely free man.

Mark showed up at her door two hours later. He had on blue jeans, an expensive leather vest, a matching button-down shirt, and cowboy boots. He looked good and sexy. Patricia was taken by Mark's looks, his actions, his attitude, and what he said to her. She had been attracted to him from the minute she met him. He had a way of carrying himself that made it clear that he was a very successful man. "How could she not love him?" she asked herself.

Patricia was wearing her favorite blue jeans and a blue cashmere sweater, and she had on a pair of high-heeled boots. She looked elegant and sexy, and Mark was truly fascinated by her. He thought she was gorgeous, and he had told her that the minute he laid eyes on her.

They drove for five hours until they came to a row of elegant shopping stores. "Do you want to stop here?" Mark asked Patricia.

"Yes, I would love to," Patricia answered. They shopped, and Patricia bought several things. Mark also bought a few choice items. Patricia picked out a few sweaters she liked, as well as two cardigans, a dress, two pairs of jeans, a couple of button-down shirts, a handbag, and a watch.

After they were done shopping, they went out to eat. They both had steak, baked potatoes, and a salad and apple pie for dessert. Afterward, they walked through the park, hand in hand, and Mark caught Patricia by surprise when he pulled her close and kissed her ever so gently. They were falling for each other at a rapid pace. Going through a nearby museum, they chatted openly with one another as they went. They seemed to have a lot in common. Then they went to a nearby bar at the Country Club Inn, and they ordered mixed drinks. They had an excellent time together. Life as it was right now couldn't be better, they thought.

It was about three o'clock in the morning when they picked out a motel room and checked in. It turned out to be a wonderful day, and the two of them were comfortable with one another. As they sat on the sofa, one thing led to another, and they were both longing for each other. Mark started to undress Patricia, and she, in turn, started undressing Mark, and before they knew it, they were having hot, passionate sex right there on the sofa, and then in the bedroom time and time again.

After making love several times, they lay spent, and they fell asleep in one another's arms until morning. It felt good to both of them to have someone in their lives after so long.

In the morning, when they woke up, they made love several times and ordered room service. They had eggs, toast, bacon, and coffee. "I hate to see our time end so soon," they both seemed to say, looking into one another's eyes. As they showered, they made love, and they got dressed afterward. Patricia put on a pair of leggings, a tunic sweater, and her high-heeled shoes, and Mark put on a sweater and his blue jeans and cowboy boots.

On their travels home, they chatted back and forth endlessly, and they stopped at several different places. "I guess it's back to work as usual tomorrow," Mark said.

"I had a wonderful time this weekend," Patricia told Mark.

"We'll do it again soon," Mark said. "Maybe in two weeks, we'll take nine or ten days and go to Vegas," Mark told her.

"I would like that very much," she said in reply.

The two said their good-byes, and the day ended on a happy but sad note.

Chapter 18

In the morning, Page woke up early. The twins were up, and they both had a fever. They seemed to have gotten sick in the past few days. They were both crying and upset. Page gave them infant medication that their pediatrician told her to give to them to treat this sickness.

Since it was so early in the morning, Page went back to bed after tending to the twins.

"What's going on?" Blake asked.

"Oh, it's the twins. They were crying, so I gave them a dose of their medicine."

"Go back to bed, and try to get some more sleep," Blake said.

"Yeah, that sounds like a good idea," Page said. "I am tired, and besides that, there is no need to be up at this time of day."

Later that morning, Patricia called Page and filled her in about her new romantic relationship. "Oh, I'm happy for you, Mom," Page told her. "The twins have the flu and were up half the night, and I feel like a zombie this morning, but other than that, everything is good with us," Page said.

"Things are moving quite rapidly between Mark and I, and he just got a divorce not long ago," Patricia said to Page.

That concerned Page, but she didn't let that on to her mother. Page didn't want her mom to feel empty again with yet another loss. "Well, Mom, just take one day at a time, and move with caution," Page told her.

Patricia didn't let on to Page that she and Mark had already gone all the way. She kept it to herself. "Well, I'll let you go," Patricia told Page.

"Thanks for calling," Page said, and then she hung up.

"What did your mom have to say?" Blake asked her.

"Oh, she was telling me all about Mark and how they went away for the weekend. I didn't want to upset her, but I'm concerned that things are moving kind of fast, especially since he just recently got a divorce from his wife. I didn't want to upset her, so I'm keeping my feelings mute." "Some things are better left unsaid," Blake told her.

"I hope she doesn't get hurt," Page said.

"Yeah, I can see where you're coming from," Blake said.

"Who knows where this will go from here."

"I think your mom is kind of blinded by the light, and I don't think she knows Mark well enough," Blake said.

"Oh well, she is old enough to make her own decisions. She will make up her mind, regardless of what we say. We can't stop her," Page replied.

"For now, let's focus on us," Blake told Page.

After making love, Page and Blake fell asleep in each other's arms.

Chapter 19

The morning started early, as usual. Blake was up and about, doing his usual chores, and Page was making breakfast for her family and tending to the twins. They were getting over being sick, and Page was very happy about that.

Blake was looking to purchase the beach home he had spoken of earlier. He had found one in their price range, and he was ready to make a down payment on it.

Page was in agreement about this. She instantly fell in love with the one they had their eyes on. "I love everything about it," she said. "I love the way it is set up. It has a wonderful view of the ocean, and it is very spacious, just the right size for us!" Page exclaimed. It was like a dream come true. It had everything imaginable, and they agreed to purchase it.

"Let's spend a night there," Blake said after they had made a down payment on it.

"Yeah, I'm game for that," Page said.

When Blake and Page arrived in Florida, the two of them rented a small boat and went for a ride out on the ocean. They talked endlessly, and they had a really good time. Things were very good between them. After that, they went for a walk on the sand. "I'm so in love with you," Blake told Page. Then they went back to the beach house, where they made love with each other. They were hungry after all their lovemaking, so then they ordered a pizza, a salad, breadsticks, and drinks. The pizza-delivery guy was at their beach house within half an hour. Blake paid for the pizza and gave him a generous tip.

After they had eaten dinner, Page and Blake sat on the couch. Blake started undressing Page, and they made love, first on the sofa and then in bed, time and time again. They fell asleep in one another's arms.

What Page didn't know was how Blake was going to turn on her. If only she knew what was going to happen just around the corner, she wouldn't have agreed to purchase this home away from home.

The next morning, Blake and Page awoke together, and they made love first thing that morning.

After that, Page got deeply involved in her work, and she didn't spend a lot of time with Blake. What she didn't realize was that this made Blake feel left out of her life. He tried to fill the void, but he didn't have any luck. Page didn't think about how lonely Blake. Their relationship was dead, as far as Blake was concerned.

What Page didn't know was that Blake was starting to talk to another woman. He called her quire frequently while Page wasn't around.

Chapter 20

One day, out of the blue, Blake suggested to Laura, the woman he was talking to, that she come to the beach house, and he would meet her there. "Page is working all the time, and she doesn't have any time for me," Blake told Laura.

"Yeah, I know what that is like," Laura said. "I've had the same kind of relationship in the past. My ex and I were together for a very short period of time. My ex started going to the bar all the time, and he went out with everything that turned him on."

"I can't believe how blind he was," Blake responded.

"Scott and I have a baby girl. Her name is Faith. She's three years old now, and I have no time at all for her daddy, but I love Faith dearly."

"Some people are like that: they'll lead you to think that they love you, and then they'll break your heart," Blake told her. What Blake was not thinking about was how stupid he was acting toward Page. How could he be so cold to her? He was doing the exact same thing to Page that he was telling Laura he didn't agree with.

Chapter 21

Blake and Laura met at the beach house the next day. They drank a little too much, one thing led to another, and before they knew it, they were in bed, making out.

What Blake didn't know was that Page would find out that he was cheating on her. He would eat his actions and his words, as he was due to find out.

At the end of the next day, Page got out of work a little earlier than usual, so she went to clean the beach house. She had the next few days off, so she decided to make up lost time with Blake.

When Page got to the beach house, she figured that she would start by cleaning the bedroom and then work from there. She was completely shocked when she saw the unthinkable. Walking into the bedroom, she saw a woman's bra and other undergarments strung over a chair. *How can this be?* Page told herself. *This can't be.* She tried to put it out of her mind, thinking to herself that it wasn't worth ruining the time that she was going to have with Blake. She tried hard to forget about it until she saw the watch that she had bought for Blake's birthday lying on the nightstand.

Oh, how stupid is he, she thought. That son of a bitch. Then, at the same time, she thought, I must be pretty stupid too. I mean, after all, something along these lines happened once before, or it's been happening over and over, and I've been blind. It blew her mind. How could she face Blake knowing all this?

Page tried to avoid the subject that night when she went home and talked to Blake; however, he was asking to be told off. His attitude was very negative. He acted as if she didn't even exist anymore.

"Okay, Blake, keep it up!" she yelled at him.

"What brought this on?" he asked.

"Oh, I cleaned the beach house last night before I came home," she replied. "While I was there, I found this." As she said this, she handed Blake the watch she had found.

"Oh, that!" he explained. "I forgot that the last time you and I were there."

"Oh, really! Then explain to me about the woman's undergarments. We've only had the beach house a short time. I guess that is the biggest mistake we've ever made," Page said. "We never should have purchased it." Page was at the point of yelling; she and Blake bickered back and forth. "Why didn't you say to me that I mean absolutely nothing to you?" Page yelled at Blake. At that, Blake tried to tell Page that he was sorry this had happened, and he tried to calm her down. "Let's make amends," he said.

"I don't think so," she answered. "I don't think after this that I'll be needing you," she said. She was in tears by now, but she wasn't giving in. What was going to happen was going to happen, and as far as Page was concerned, it was over between them. It was probably for the best, she thought.

Blake realized that he had really screwed up, but he couldn't go back now.

The past can't be reversed, and their marriage was in danger.

Chapter 22

Blake did everything he could possibly think of to try to make it up to Page. She wouldn't give in at first, but she was lonely, and she needed someone in her life. Her instincts told her not to let him manipulate her, but she knew him all too well, and she knew that when it came to Blake, he would win her back all over again.

Time flew by quickly. A whole month passed before Blake and Page knew it. Things between them started to improve. They spent almost two weeks at the beach house and endless time together.

The phone rang one afternoon. Laura was on the line. Blake answered, and what she said shocked him. Laura told him that she was pregnant. She said that she was a little over a month late. "Oh, how can that be?" Blake asked in an angry tone. "We only went all the way once, and you're telling me that you're knocked up? You told me you were on the pill." "I must have forgotten to take it that day," Laura said.

"Oh, now this whole thing is really getting stupid," Blake told Laura. "How could I have been so foolish and fallen for your stupid line, telling me you were on the pill?"

At that point, Page got out of the shower and walked into the room. "Who was on the phone?" she asked.

"Oh, it was no one—just someone trying to sell stuff," Blake said quickly, and he hung up the phone.

Blake was between a rock and a hard spot. He tried to put it all out of his mind and focus on Page and himself, but the secret was eating at him, and it was going to continue eating at him. He would never be able to explain it all to Page. How could he? His actions were speaking louder than his words were.

Page sensed that there was something wrong, as Blake's lovemaking wasn't nearly as intense as it usually was.

Time flew by all too quickly, and before they knew it, it was back to business as usual.

Chapter 23

Patricia came over to the house that afternoon. It was the Fourth of July, and Blake and Page had invited everyone to their house for a celebration. Mark was stopping by a little later, as he had some other things to tend to first.

When Mark did show up at the house, he told Patricia what she really didn't want to hear. "I got a call from the hospital early this morning. Kelly was in a pretty bad accident, and they didn't know whether she was going to pull through or not. I guess I owe it to her to take care of the kids and help her while she's recovering."

"It's too bad about your wife," Patricia said.

At the same time, Patricia thought, where in the world does this leave me? Mark is going to be with Kelly constantly, and it leaves me out of the picture. It will only get worse before it gets any better.

That day, everyone at Blake and Page's house felt bad for what Mark was going through, and they knew that it was going to hurt Patricia.

Patricia didn't have much to say following Mark's news about Kelly. Observing Page's and Blake's actions, Patricia sensed that something else was wrong. Blake knew in his heart that there was no explaining what had happened between him and Laura to Page. He figured that his marriage was over.

Mark left the party early, as he was concerned about Kelly and wanted to go to the hospital to see her. When he got to the hospital, he was relieved to see that she was holding her own. Mark talked to Dr. Morgan and the nurses working at the time.

Dr. Morgan said that Kelly was lucky to be alive. He said that she had lost her sight completely because shattered glass had gotten into her eyes and face, but she wouldn't realize it until she came to. "Her face is also pretty badly bruised and beaten," Dr. Morgan said, "and her right arm is broken, but other than that, she survived."

The fact that Kelly had lost her sight devastated Mark; he said that he would take her to as many eye doctors as possible to try to fix the problem.

He stayed at the hospital all day. He continually stroked Kelly's hair and talked to her, the doctor, and the staff, who said that his presence would help Kelly's condition as much as the medicine that they were giving to her. Mark knew that, when she did come around, she would not be happy with her condition.

At the end of the day, Mark called Patricia and let her know how Kelly was doing. Patricia said that she was sorry to hear about Kelly; she knew that this would mean the end of her relationship with Mark. She would be free again, although she really didn't want to be. One day, she was happy and she seemingly had everything, and the next day, she was down on her luck. Fate doesn't add up most of the time, or so it seemed.

Oh well, she thought, I'm still young, and the prospects of someone else coming around are still good.

Chapter 24

Mark called Patricia from time to time, but he stayed mostly involved with helping Kelly. She needed him dearly, and as far as Patricia was concerned, she always would. Patricia would always be Mark's second choice—just someone to vent to. It was over with Mark, in Patricia's eyes. She talked to him when he called, only to help him through tough times. This would remain their only contact now. What they had before was almost forgotten.

Patricia only went through the motions now. Down the road, maybe someone else would find her, or she would find someone—that is, if she even cared anymore, at her age. She was starting to think not.

Blake was still trying to act as if he only loved Page, but Page knew all too well that this wasn't so.

If only I could go back and reverse my actions, Blake thought.

Laura called him several times, but each time, Blake refused to give in to her wishes. He only said, "How do you know it's my kid?"

She always said, "You are the only guy I was with."

"Yeah right, that's what they all say," Blake replied. "Our relationship—if you can even call it a relationship—is over and done with." Blake wished that he could believe the baby wasn't his. *If only I hadn't screwed up,* was all Blake could think, and it wasn't doing his and Page's relationship one bit of good. How stupid things were turning out, and it was all because of him.

Page's birthday was in two days, so Blake purchased a diamond bracelet with which to surprise her. Since Page's birthday fell in July, Blake bought a cut diamond bracelet with rubies, her birthstone, as well as a beautiful peach faux-fur cardigan. He also took her out to dinner.

Their romance was starting to bloom again, but in the back of Blake's mind, he thought that it would probably be over soon. Blake called Laura one day while Page was out, and he told her not to call his house anymore. He said that, if he had to, he would pay child support. "Other than that, don't expect anything from me," he told her.

Chapter 25

Now, Patricia was alone. Mark's constant attention on Kelly had left a void in her life. She wasn't sure if she should ever fall for another man telling her that she was the one he loved. She expected that it wasn't worth getting hurt again. In many ways, she was afraid that she would love and lose. But nothing in any relationship could be as devastating as the death of John, the father of her children.

Patricia still asked herself why. Why did he die so young? My grandchildren didn't even get to know their grandpa. His death made a bad situation for the entire family, most of all for me. I guess life's ups and downs make the world go around, Patricia thought.

Kelly had been home for a little more than a month, and Patricia hadn't heard from Mark since. *I guess I've talked to him for the last time,* Patricia thought. Then, that evening, around seven o'clock, the phone rang, and Patricia was surprised to hear Mark's voice on the line.

"Kelly is okay," he said, "but she is not happy about having no eyesight. I've told her over and over that she is very lucky to be alive. Life isn't always fair, I've told her, and she forfeited her eyesight for her life. She just doesn't understand it all yet. How have you been?" Mark asked Patricia.

"Well, I'm lonely. Other than that, I'm fine," she told him.

"I'm sorry to hear that," Mark said, "and I'm sorrier still that I can't be with you. I owe it to Kelly now, after all this, and she will get my full attention."

Patricia thought that he was being very blunt, and she felt like asking him why he had bothered to call, but she kept her emotions to herself. Mark was all but out of her life now. What Patricia and Mark had between them just felt like a mere fling now.

How stupid could I be? Patricia thought. Maybe I'm better off without someone in my life. They say everything turns out for the better, and Mark did leave me standing alone, when it was all said and done.

Patricia felt alone that night as she climbed into bed and fell asleep. What she didn't know was that Page, too, felt alone, although she had Blake. *I guess love doesn't last forever, like I once thought,* Patricia said to herself.

Chapter 26

Page phoned Patricia the next morning at nine o'clock. The two women decided to spend the day together shopping.

Page was ready when Patricia arrived at her house that morning. She had on leggings, a tunic sweater, and knee-high boots. Patricia had on jeans, a yellow sweater, and boots. She looked nice; yellow seemed to be her color, and Page told her so. Patricia also carried a handbag that she got many compliments on every time she took it out with her. It was black and adorned with red hearts. It was very appropriate on this day, as it was the day before Valentine's Day.

Daughter and mother had a wonderful time as they shopped endlessly. Page purchased a red sweater dress with white snowflakes knit into it, a pair of jeans, and two lightweight sweaters, one peach with an Aztec print in the center and one dark blue, which many women said was her color. She also purchased a couple of fragrances, some socks, and a pair of dress shoes, which she instantly loved. Patricia bought several items as well, including a couple of new spring dresses, a few shirts, and a handbag that Page loved. She also purchased a pair of sandals to go with her dresses.

The two of them stopped to eat on their way home. They each ordered a chicken salad with rolls, which they ate very little of, and cocktails. The two women talked endlessly about everything, from what a good time they had had shopping to the men in their lives.

Patricia told Page that her relationship with Mark looked bleak. "He went back to Kelly," she said.

"That's too bad. I feel for you, Mom. But don't lose hope; someone better will come into your life," Page said.

"Yeah, I'm trying to believe that," Patricia said.

"I'm having trouble in my relationship with Blake as well," Page said. "He is cheating on me, and he denies it all the time. I'm all but ready to move on also."

"I'm so sorry to hear that," Patricia said. "I didn't realize how bad it was between you two. Hang in there, if possible," Patricia said. "You have been working extra hard with the business and the children."

"Yeah, I have, Mom, but he doesn't have to act like this. And, besides, it isn't just that he's having an affair. I believe that he has something else going on, which he refuses to let me in on. The phone has rung many times, and Blake will talk to the person on the line. Then I inquire as to who's on the line, and I get a reply, but I don't get a direct answer—only what Blake believes sounds good. I don't know what it is, but I can read Blake like a book. I can sense when he's making things up and when he's telling me the truth."

"Well, it sounds like something has gone wrong in both of our relationships," Patricia said, and both women agreed.

"Well, it's getting late in the day," Page told her mom. "I guess I better get home, as I have a big week planned, and I'm going to try to forget about everything that has gone wrong between Blake and me. I mean, after all, he does try to make our relationship exciting. I can't prove anything yet, anyway, so why stir up a hornet's nest?" Page said.

The two women returned home, laughing, talking, and feeling carefree again, which didn't happen often in either of their lives. "We'll have to do this again soon," they agreed, and that night, they went to bed with carefree thoughts.

Chapter 27

Blake's life was really getting screwed up, as far as he was concerned. Page said that she thought she was pregnant again, because she had missed her monthly. That meant that Laura, who had just been a one-night fling, and Page, whom he deeply cared about and whom he had a very good relationship with, were both pregnant. How stupid his life was turning out to be.

How could he explain it all to Page? He knew that there was no good explanation for his actions. Now, he really felt as if he had made a mistake, and he wanted to go back to that one-night fling and change things, but he couldn't. *You can't change this bad of a mistake,* Blake thought. He knew that he would have to pay when it was all said and done; he felt it.

Page was the person who would suffer most of all because of him. He owed everything good in his life to her, and she was in a motherly way again, so he was going to pay dearly, he realized.

Page made an appointment to see her gynecologist. He confirmed what she already suspected: she was seven weeks along. Everything looked good, the doctor assured her.

"I don't think I want to have twins this time," Page said, laughing.

"Yeah, I don't think you need to worry about that," the doctor said.

Page went home and told Blake what was already expected. "I'm seven weeks into my pregnancy."

"Well, Mrs. Turner, we better start taking precautions from now on after this."

"Yeah, I agree, although making babies is fun. They're just hard to support."

"Yeah, they do take an awful lot," Blake replied.

Page called her mom and told her the news.

"Oh, I'm happy for you and Blake," Patricia said.

"The doctor confirmed that there is no need to worry about twins this time," Page told her mom. "Blake is happy, but he acted as if he doesn't want any more kids after this."

"Well, four children between the ages of four and two and then one on the way is an awful lot to manage," Page's mom said. "Then there is your business to operate on a daily basis. All of this needs to be considered."

"The business is really running quite well," Page said. "Blake is helping out when I need him. He does a lot of the ordering, and he does the maintenance to keep costs down."

"It's good that he is taking the initiative to do all that," Patricia said.

"We'll need the extra income, as the new baby will take it," Page said.

The days and weeks flew by very quickly, as they have a tendency to do. Laura called Blake a few times after he told her not to call again. One morning, she called to tell Blake that they had had a boy, and she was going to name him Shawn Paul. She said that the baby would have her last name: London. At least that turned out well. Blake never told Page anything about this.

Page and Blake's baby was due at any time. They were having a girl, and Page was undecided on what to name her. She liked the name Faith Lynn and thought she might go with that.

Labor came on very quickly this time, and they had a healthy baby girl because of it.

Page decided to name their new baby Faith, as she had brought up earlier, and Blake agreed, saying that he loved the name as well.

"I love you just as much now as I ever have, Page," Blake told his wife, "Maybe more. You are everything I've ever wanted in a woman.

You are very successful in your business, and you always have been, since the first day I met you."

"I love you as much, Blake. You are a wonderful husband, and you've always done everything possible to see that life is exciting for me. Call my mom, Blake, and tell her I had a baby girl. She will be happy."

"Hello, Patricia," Blake said when he called Page's mother and she answered. "We're here at the hospital. Page just had a baby girl, and she named her Faith. Mother and baby are doing quite well."

"That is very good news," Patricia said. "I'll be there as soon as possible. I want to see my new granddaughter."

When Patricia walked into the room, she hugged her daughter. "Hi, Page, how are you doing?"

"I'm doing very well," Page told her mother. "I couldn't be better, considering the circumstances. This time, everything went well."

"Everything sounds good," Patricia told Page.

Blake brought Taylor and the twins in to see their new sister. Taylor saw her mom and asked, "Are you okay, Mom?" "Yeah, I'm doing fine," Page answered.

At the end of the day, after everyone had left, the doctor said that everything looked good and he would check on her the next day to see if she looked ready to go home.

In the morning, hospital staff brought Page her breakfast. She had eggs, bacon, toast, and coffee. She was hungry, so she ate everything.

When the doctor came into the room, he remarked on her good appetite and said that it was a good sign that she was healing well. He decided to keep Page one more day, since they didn't discharge people on Sundays.

Blake called Page to see how she was, and she said that she would be home the next day.

"Oh, that sounds good to me," Blake told her.

The nursery was all set up and ready for the new baby when Page got home. She was up most of that first night.

Chapter 28

Faith turned out to be a really good baby. After the first couple of months, she started sleeping through the night. She grew fast, gaining three pounds in the first two months.

Page was getting deep into her work at the Western Shop, and she had her hands full with her children too. The new baby was partly Blake's responsibility, and he did a good job helping out.

"What do you say we go to the beach house for the week?" Blake asked Page one day.

"I would enjoy that very much," Page said. "I could use a break from all this work with the shop and all the family life. I need some quality time alone with you, Blake. I suggest that we proceed with caution, though, because I really don't want to get pregnant again, at least not this soon."

"Yeah, I agree that it would be a bit soon. We don't want to get pregnant every time we have sex," Blake said.

At that, the two of them laughed. They truly did seem to understand each other, which is oftentimes missing among married couples. *If Page only knew the whole story about Laura and me, she would probably divorce my ass,* Blake thought to himself.

Blake and Page packed the next day. They had to get someone to watch the babies. They both thought that time away would do them a world of good. Little did they know that the trip was going to turn out to be a mistake and almost wreck their marriage.

Page packed several pairs of shorts, tank tops, jeans, a couple of sweaters for cooler weather, and a few pairs of flip-flops and three swimsuits, which she had purchased the past summer. She always kept a supply of them, as she never knew when they would go to the beach house. Besides that, she wanted to look sexy for Blake.

Blake thought she looked terrific, and he told her so quite frequently. She was thirty-five years old, but he would remark that she didn't look a day more than twenty. Page laughed at his remarks, but she thought it very good that she still turned him on just by being naked.

When she wore sundresses and short-shorts, Blake told her that if she kept looking this good, she would be out of her clothes and in bed, in his arms. Blake loved flattering her, and she loved his comments. The things Blake said, the times when he chose to say them, and the way they made her feel were all well worth it. The two kids, as a lot of people referred to them, were happy knowing that they were getting away for a little while, and they felt like kids because of it.

When they got to the beach house, the first thing on the agenda was to take care of each other, and they melted into each other's arms. How good life was when they spent quality time together. As they lay in bed, Blake told Page how good she looked. She kissed him, one thing led to another, and then they were engaging in hot, passionate sex until they couldn't get enough of each other.

"I love you, Page, just as much now as I ever did before, and in many ways more so, because we have been through a lot together," Blake told her. After their lovemaking, they showered, got dressed, and went out to eat. As they ate, they talked on and on, and they truly enjoyed one another's company.

"I love you, Page," Blake said. "You are the sexiest woman I know." They were in love, and it showed. "Life is good right now when I'm with you." "Yeah, I agree. Life is good when we are together," Page replied.

At the end of the day, the two of them rented a sailboat and went out on the water. They talked endlessly as Blake held Page, and afterward, they fell asleep at the beach house and held each other as they slept.

Chapter 29

Blake and Page slept at the beach house that night, and in the morning, when Blake woke up, he went out for a walk on the sand up the coast. When Page woke up, she wondered where Blake was. Then she turned on the light and opened up the nightstand drawer. When she did, she couldn't believe what she saw. Inside the drawer was a letter. It read,

Dear Blake,

I was at the beach house earlier today. I miss you badly, and I'd really like to see you again. I miss what we had, and I would like to be with you.

Our baby boy is almost three months old now, and he is really a handful. I've told him about you. I realize he is too young to know the difference right now, but in the future, he'll want to know who his dad is, and I want him to know you.

I know you told me not to bother calling or trying to get in touch with you, but I'm lonely, and I need you to fill the void in my life.

I still love you, and I have feelings for you. I want very badly to see you again, and I want you to see Shawn and spend quality father–son time with him. After all, you are his dad. I feel that you at least owe it to Shawn to spend some time with him.

That one night at the beach house really changed my life, and I will never forget you. I really do love you with all my heart. Please call me and keep in touch.

Laura

How stupid is Blake? And how stupid am I? Page asked herself. *Blake has been unfaithful to me, and I fell for his lies, telling me that*

no one was on the line when she was calling the house. Page was fuming by now. She was unsure what she wanted to say to Blake.

When Blake did return from his walk, Page met him at the door, and she handed him the letter, screaming at him.

"You stupid son of a bitch!" she said to him. "You have been fucking other women! Why didn't you tell me you had a son with someone else? Now I know I'm just another piece of ass to you and I mean nothing to you.

Maybe we should just call it quits, get a divorce, and go our separate ways." "Are you finished bitching at me?" Blake asked.

"What do you think?" Page asked Blake.

"Well, I would say that, by the sound of it, I won't hear the end of all this," Blake told her.

"I would say that, in this case, that is correct," Page said.

Their time at the beach house was ending on an unhappy note. "Well, we could stay longer," Blake said, "but I don't want to hear any more about Laura and me and the son you knew nothing about."

"You are absolutely thick skulled, Blake Turner!" Page shouted. "You act as if you don't have a brain and as if I'm supposed to give in every time something stupid happens. This beach house was a mistake—I said it before, and I'll say it again."

"Yeah, I hear you loud and clear," Blake said. "Could you please keep your voice down? I don't want all the people on the beach to know our business."

As Page packed, she threw her clothes into her suitcase, and she continued to give Blake hell.

"Well, this whole week turned out to be a big mistake," Blake said to Page.

"Yeah, thanks to you and your stupidity!" Page yelled.

"Are you done yelling yet?" Blake asked.

"I don't think so. I'm not going to let you live this down," Page said.

"Are you telling me that it is over between us?" Blake asked, trying to patch up what was left.

"Right now, the way I feel, yes, I do," Page said. "What do you think?" she added.

"Yelling isn't going to change things or make them any better," Blake said, trying to calm Page down.

"Boy, now I know how stupid and thickheaded you are," Page said. "I don't know if I'm getting through to you or not!" she screamed.

Blake knew, in his heart of hearts, that he would never again have the kind of relationship with Page that he once had, and he resented that dearly. He also thought to himself that she may not want him after all this was said and done. He thought that he would be lucky if she even gave him the time of day after he had screwed up so badly.

"You act as if I don't matter anymore," Page replied.

The worst possible result had come true. Blake wanted to take back what he had done. He wanted Page the way he used to have Page—carefree and head over heels in love—but he knew that was never going to happen again, not in a million years.

Page was subdued and cold in bed, to say the least. It was going to take a miracle to get Page back, and Blake knew it.

Chapter 30

Page called her mom and asked if she was game for another shopping trip. The two of them decided to go that Saturday.

Page hadn't talked to her mom in a while; therefore, she had a lot to tell her. Page was one of those daughters who confides in her mom about mostly everything. "I have a story to tell you, Mom, but I'm going to tell you in person."

"Okay," Patricia responded. "I have a new love in my life."

"Oh, really, Mom, how wonderful!" Page answered. "Who is the lucky man this time?"

"Oh, his name is Timothy Lambert, and he is a lawyer. He has been divorced for five years," Patricia said.

"I hope he isn't as bad as Mark was, and I hope he doesn't break your heart like Mark did," Page told her mom.

"Yeah, Timothy has five children. He has three girls and two boys. All of his children are older, from ages twenty-two to seventeen."

"What does his ex-do?" Page asked. "I hope she doesn't work at his law firm."

"No, she is a nurse, and she has absolutely nothing to do with Timothy," Patricia told Page.

"I'm hoping you are right this time, for your own sake, because you said pretty much the same stuff about Mark, and he went straight back to his ex. Where did you and Timothy meet?" Page inquired.

"Actually, we met at the bar one night. At the end of the night, we wound up at his apartment," Patricia said. She didn't need to be told to be cautious or to not get too extreme. At this point, she had no idea what her daughter was going through with Blake.

"Well, I'll see you on Saturday, Mom," Page said. "I'll have Blake watch the kids so we can enjoy the day."

"That sounds good to me," Patricia said.

"Yeah, we need time alone," Patricia and Page both agreed.

The two women laughed, saying it must be true, as they had both said it at the same time. Patricia and Page had an excellent relationship. Two women couldn't get along better if they tried.

When Page got off the phone, Blake acted as if he wanted sex. He pulled Page close and whispered into her ear. He usually got his way with her, as it was just the way he was.

The two of them wound up making out in bed together, but they weren't nearly as close as they had once been. Blake felt awful because of it. He could sense the tension between them.

Page stayed deeply involved in running the Western Shop, and it was going quite well. She had just hired two girls, as the Christmas season was upon them—just two months away—and she needed the additional staff. The girls whom she hired had a lot of fashion knowledge.

Page ordered a whole line of Aztec-patterned coats, shirts, dresses, purses, and shoes of all colors for the holiday season. Page loved all the colors of the rainbow—pink, purple, blue, yellow, red, and orange—and then some. A lot of women loved what she ordered; it sold like hotcakes, so Page's business was booming.

The store was the talk of the town, so, along with Christmas, which was fast approaching, sales would be booming and business never better. It meant extra orders and different items they usually didn't sell, and it also meant a bigger staff because of the added sales. Everything was worth it in the end, because it all meant success.

Page and Blake were starting to get along again. Page thought that she could forgive Blake, because she had a kind heart, but his affair with Laura would remain on her mind. Blake would pay for his action for the rest of his life.

Everything seemed to become fairly normal again until the phone rang one day and Page answered it.

"Hello?" Page said.

"Yes, hello, is Blake there?" the person on the other end said.

"Yeah, he is here. Who is calling?" Page asked, somewhat puzzled, but in the back of her mind, she knew who it was already.

Laura just told her, "Someone who wants to talk to Blake."

Page told Blake that he had a phone call, and she also said that it was a woman.

"Hello," Laura said when Blake got to the phone.

"What's up?" Blake asked Laura.

"Oh, not much. It's just lonely here when I haven't heard from you in so long. Shawn is really getting big," Laura said. "He looks just like you, Blake. We ought to set up a time so you can see your son." Laura really knew how to put Blake on the spot. "Where would you like to meet so you can at least see Shawn?"

Laura is pretty thick skulled, Blake was thinking to himself. "I'm not at all sure if I should get involved, Laura," Blake said.

"Well, I'll let you go, Blake," Laura told him. "I'll call again soon."

Blake thought, you don't need to call again, but, on the other hand, he thought, Shawn is partly my responsibility. What a mix-up. Then Blake said, "I've got to go."

Laura thought that he was cold in many ways. "I'll keep in touch with you," Laura told Blake.

"Oh, I'm sure you will," Blake said.

Then the conversation ended with Laura telling Blake how in love with him she still was. "I'll always be in love with you," Laura told Blake.

With a blank look on his face, Blake stood up, knowing he would never hear the end of it and that her feelings were mostly his fault.

"Was that Laura on the phone?" Page asked.

"Yeah, it was," Blake answered.

Page considered getting angry, but it wouldn't solve the problem. Besides, Blake always seemed to get his way with her in the end. What had happened between Blake and Laura was a mistake; it never should have happened, but there was now a new life because of it. Page thought that she should either get a divorce or try to get along with Blake. Considering the circumstances, what else could she do? She decided to try to get along with Blake. She figured that it would be best for both of them.

Page decided to make amends. After all, she thought, he may have a little boy to another woman, but it is still his.

Chapter 31

When they awoke the next morning, Blake pulled Page over to him, and he fondled her breasts until she couldn't stand it any longer. He went over every inch of her body, exploring her, and then they made love over and over again. It got intense again, just as their lovemaking had been before Page knew about Laura.

Blake once again felt like a lucky man, feeling past all the conflict he had gone through with Laura and Page. Blake had figured that his marriage to Page was over and that it would end in a bitter divorce. From now on, Blake would take everything more seriously. He would do all that he could to take care of Page.

Page's mother called to see if her daughter was still in the mood to go shopping, as planned.

"Yeah, I'm getting Blake and the kids their breakfast, and then I'm going to bathe and get ready myself."

When Patricia got there, Page was ready. She wore a pair of her favorite blue jeans and a button-up shirt in red plaid. She had on her gray distressed leather jacket and gray knee-high boots. She looked very pretty. Page always took excellent care of her body, and it showed. She had the body of a twenty-year-old woman at thirty-six years old. Page believed in eating healthily, and she thought that it would contribute to a wonderful body, along with exercise and a positive attitude—all that, plus Page had a pretty face, which added to her youthfulness. She was an elegant woman.

Patricia was pretty as well; it was easy to see where Page got her good looks. Patricia was also dressed in jeans, as well as a black denim shirt, tan knee-high boots, and a tan distressed-leather coat, one of the more elegant clothing items Patricia owned. Together, the two women spelled gorgeous.

The women hit all the stores on the boulevard of interest to them. The Christmas crowds were hustling and bustling, and the stores were full of people shopping for special gifts. The Christmas season brought out the best in people, as everyone was kind and cheerful.

Page and her mom shopped at the Western Shop as well as other stores. Page tried on a couple of dresses and some jeans, shirts, and shoes. Patricia also tried on some different items of clothing as well as some shoes. Both women spent a lot of money. Page purchased two dresses, a pair of jeans, two shirts, a purse, and a pair of shoes. Patricia purchased a dress, two pairs of jeans, two shirts, a purse, and a black distressed-leather coat, which she instantly loved.

The two women had a wonderful time, and when they were finished shopping, they went out to dinner. Patricia had a porterhouse steak, a baked potato with sour cream and butter, a salad, and tea to drink. Patricia had a stuffed chicken breast, a baked potato, a salad, and sweet tea also.

Page confided in Patricia. "Blake and I have had quite a bit of trouble lately."

"How so?" Patricia inquired.

"Oh, he had sex with another woman—Laura—and he wound up getting her pregnant," Page said. "She had a boy, and she named him Shawn. Shawn is about three months old now. Laura told Blake that Shawn looks like him. She wants Blake to meet her and spend quality time with their son."

"I wouldn't let him meet her alone," Patricia said. "I would go with him. That way, you're involved also, and you know nothing else is going to happen between Blake and Laura."

"Yeah, that is a smart idea, Mom," Page said.

The two women returned home happy and relaxed, and that night, as Page went to bed, she felt happy with the choices that she had made.

Chapter 32

The next day, Page went to the Western Shop, as she usually did. Sales were still up, partly due to the holiday season. She did her share of taking orders, and she had many special orders coming in for different individuals. A lot of the current sales were purchases from men who were trying to please their wives for Christmas with jewelry, coats, and purses, among other things.

After putting a Now Hiring sign in the shop-door window, Page had a stack of applications to choose from. At this time of year, Page was still hiring seasonal help. Some jobs would lead to full-time roles, depending on the girls' availability and such.

When Page returned home one evening after a long day's work, she found that she had received a letter. Reading it, she discovered that she had won a Caribbean cruise trip for eight days and seven nights. Page immediately called the letter's phone number and was told that the letter was absolutely right—she had won a cruise trip for two people.

"We're assuming that you and your husband will be going, is this correct, Mrs. Turner?"

"Yes, it is," Page said.

When Blake came in from feeding the horses, Page told him about the prize. "We have to take the cruise between now and next year," she said.

"Well, that can certainly be arranged," Blake said.

One thing had completely slipped Page's mind: she had missed her period. Then one day, out of the blue, she realized this, and she thought that, with her luck, she was probably pregnant. She went to the nearby drugstore to buy a test, and when she did it at home, she tested positive. *Oh my,* she thought, *I'm pregnant again.* The next day, Page made a doctor's appointment.

The doctor confirmed that she was almost eight weeks along. "You're in a motherly way again, Page," Dr. Bently told her.

When Page got home, she told Blake the news. He was happy, but he also told her that he thought she didn't want any more children.

"I hope you're not angry with me because you're pregnant again," Blake told Page.

"Oh, I'm not angry at you because I'm pregnant," Page said. "We did spend two weeks at the beach house about two months ago," Page said to Blake.

"Yeah, we did, and this is the result of it." Blake smiled as he said it.

"I'm glad you're accepting it all in stride," Page said. "I said that the beach house was our worst investment. Now, I think that it is one of our best investments, in many ways," Page said.

"You are truly a lovely woman in *all* ways, Page," Blake replied.

"Yes, and I love you very much," Page told Blake.

Thanksgiving was only a week away. Patricia told the family that she would do the cooking and have Thanksgiving at her house. Patricia called Page, saying, "I'm having Timothy here as well. It will give all the family a chance to meet him," as Blake walked in.

"Who's on the phone?" Blake asked Page.

"Oh, it's my mom," Page told Blake.

Then Patricia said that Timothy had proposed marriage and that she had accepted.

"That's wonderful news, Mom," Page told her. "I couldn't be happier for you. You need a man in your life again."

"Yeah, he is a little like your dad, in many ways," Patricia said. "Your dad, however, will never be replaced in my heart of hearts."

"Well, I'll bring a covered dish. That way, you don't have to do all the cooking," Page said. "By the way, I'm pregnant again. I'm about eight weeks along."

"Another grandchild on the way. I'm happy if you are, Page," Patricia said.

"Well, Mom, if I don't talk to you before Thanksgiving, then I'll talk to you then," Page said.

After Page and her mom got off the phone, Blake suggested that they go to a nearby restaurant for dinner.

"I'm game for that," Page told Blake.

"First, I want to take advantage of your body," Blake said.

Blake and Page had sex first in bed, then in the shower. Afterward, Page got dressed. She wore a dress, and she looked so good that Blake thought he wanted her once again. Page looked good, regardless of what she was wearing.

"You're glowing," Blake told her.

Page merely laughed at his comment. "I wonder why," she said, once they got to the restaurant. They each got the salad bar and a steak and a baked potato. They talked endlessly, as they always did.

"I think, after Thanksgiving is over, we should go to the beach house for a week," Blake said.

"Well, I won't need to worry about getting pregnant this time," Page replied.

Thanksgiving arrived before they knew it. Every year, it seemed as if the holidays came a little quicker.

Patricia introduced Timothy to everyone in the family. Page thought that he seemed very nice. Patricia needed someone like him to fill the void in her life.

The family had a good Thanksgiving, and they all talked at ease, getting along and enjoying one another's company. Everyone liked Timothy, and they said so afterward. Following the meal, Patricia said that she and Timothy were planning a June wedding.

"Oh, that is wonderful, Mom." All of Patricia's family agreed. "We couldn't be happier for you."

The holiday was over before they knew it. The day after Thanksgiving, Page and Blake packed to spend the week at the beach house. Page packed shorts, tank tops, a couple of swimsuits, and some other miscellaneous items. She also packed sexy sundresses and sandals to go with them, so she would look good when they went out together. Blake packed what he wanted and what he needed to look good.

After they got done packing, Blake pulled Page close, and they had sex.

Then they showered and got dressed to go to their home away from home.

Chapter 33

On the way to the beach house, rain came down so hard that Blake could hardly see the road. The rain made the road slippery. When Blake hit a big puddle, the car spun out of control. A big tractor-trailer truck was coming straight at them. Blake couldn't see where he was going, and he hit the truck, hard on the car's driver's side.

Unfortunately, Blake died on impact. Page survived. They took her by ambulance to the nearest hospital. Hitting her head on the car's windshield, Page suffered a slight concussion. Once she was at the hospital, the staff went through her purse to find her identification. In her purse, they found her license and a picture of her mother.

"This has to be her mother," a nurse named Alice said.

"Either that or it's an older sister," Laura, another nurse, said.

Page made it through the night. When she woke up in the morning, she realized that she was in a strange place.

"Where is Blake?" she asked. She had no idea what had taken place. The nurses didn't know how to tell Page about Blake. Page again asked where he was.

Cheryl, a nurse, calmly tried to explain. "You and Blake were in a terrible accident. Your husband, Blake, didn't make it."

When the nurse said these words, Page started to cry hysterically. "No," she yelled, "that can't be!"

"I'm afraid it is," the one nurse said. Page was completely hysterical by now. She cried uncontrollably, and the nursing staff tried to calm her down. "You survived. We know you're with child, and the baby is also doing well, considering what you went through."

Page was glad about that, but she also said that the baby was Blake's child and that the baby would never know who his or her dad was.

"We are all sorry about that," the nurses said.

The nurse Laura showed Page her mother's picture and asked, "Is this your mother?"

"Yeah, it is," Page told Laura.

"Can we call her?" Laura asked.

"Yeah, that will be okay," Page told Laura.

When they got Patricia on the phone and gave her the news, she started crying instantly, and she said she would get to the hospital as soon as she could. When Patricia got to the hospital, she hugged Page, and she asked where Blake was.

Page was crying again when Patricia said Blake's name. She told Patricia that he hadn't made it; he had died instantly upon impact.

Patricia was also crying after Page told her the awful news.

"I'm sorry to hear that, Page. How awful," her mother said.

"How about the baby?" Patricia asked.

"Oh, the doctor said the baby is fine," Page said.

At that, the doctor came into the room. "Hi! I'm Dr. Gordon," he said as he extended his hand and shook Patricia's hand. "She has been through quite a trauma."

"Yes, she has," Patricia said.

"At least she is alive and it didn't seem to hurt the baby," Dr. Gordon told Patricia.

"That's good news, at least," Patricia said.

Patricia stayed into the night. They suggested that she stay at the hospital so she could be with her daughter. They brought her a chair, where she stayed and slept through the night. In the morning, they brought Page breakfast.

"I'm going to go down to the cafeteria and get something to eat myself," Patricia said.

"Yeah, go ahead," Page told her. "You're probably getting pretty hungry by now."

Patricia stayed with her daughter all the next day and night. The day after that, she went home to take a shower and get a change of clothes and something to eat.

While at home, Patricia packed enough clothes to stay at the hospital for the rest of the time that Page would be there.

On a daily basis, Dr. Gordon talked to Page and evaluated her overall health.

"How are you doing today, Page?" Dr. Gordon asked her on one of these occasions.

"I feel better today than I did before," Page answered him. "I'm feeling a little bit stronger each day."

"That sounds good. Your vitals are all very good. I will see you again tomorrow morning," he said with a smile.

He's a very nice man, Page thought, and an excellent doctor as well.

Patricia had bought Page a book and brought it to her at the hospital just before she went home so Page could fill up her time with reading. It was an excellent book, and the title couldn't be any better, considering Page's situation. It was called *My Road to Recovery*.

Patricia arrived at the hospital later that evening. As she walked into Page's room, she was happy to see that Page was reading the book that she had bought. Patricia hugged Page.

"How are you doing now?" Patricia asked.

"I feel a little better, and thank you for the book you bought for me. It's very interesting. It reminds me of my life so far." "It's good that you like it," Patricia told Page.

That evening, the two women talked back and forth with ease. The next morning, like clockwork, the staff brought in Page's breakfast. She was eating well. When Dr. Gordon did his rounds, he said to Page, "It looks like we could send you home in a few days." "That sounds good to me," Page said.

By the end of that week, Page was discharged.

She had mixed emotions about going home, since she was going home without Blake.

Patricia took Page home and stayed with her to make sure everything went well. She hugged Page and then left to go home.

That night, as Page got into bed, she was lonely for Blake. All she could say was, "Why did this all happen the way it did?" Life is truly an up-and-down road full of twists, as Patricia and Page had found out.

Chapter 34

Page slept well that night. It was ten o'clock in the morning when she got out of bed. She thought that she had slept all day and that the day was over, but, of course, she hadn't gotten home the night before until eleven o'clock, and she hadn't gone to sleep until one o'clock in the morning. She had been told to take it easy for a few days, anyway.

Patricia came to check on Page and make sure she was doing well. "I think I'm going to sell the beach house," Page announced. "I can use the extra money now, and besides that, I have no use for it without Blake."

The following week, Page had a doctor's appointment, and the doctor confirmed that she was able to resume normal activities.

Three weeks before Christmas, Patricia asked Page if she wanted to go shopping. Page said that she would go, but she told her mom that she wasn't in the holiday spirit, considering the circumstances. Patricia announced to her family that she would make the meal. Christmas just wasn't the same this year for Page. She felt a void inside herself without Blake.

New Year's Day came and went, and Page still felt lonely. Page kept busy daily with the Western Shop. Patricia talked to her daughter regularly on the phone.

Valentine's Day was soon upon them. Patricia called Page and told her that she and Timothy had a date. Timothy picked Patricia up, and they went to dinner. Patricia dressed elegantly in black slacks, a yellow sweater, and a pair of high heels. The two of them had steak, potatoes, and a fine wine. They talked about their families; their wedding, which was just around the corner; and how much they loved each other. After dinner, Timothy suggested that they go see a movie. Then they wound up going to a nearby hotel to spend the night. Timothy was unpredictable, which was one of the things that Patricia loved most about him. Another of his positive traits was keeping things fun; there was always something new in their relationship. The two of them couldn't be any more in love.

When Patricia got home the next day, she was deep in thought about her wedding preparations. She chose Page to be her maid of honor, but after much thought, Page decided that she didn't want to be in the wedding party. Patricia fully understood why Page felt this way in her condition, and following the trauma that she had gone through just months before, with the loss of her husband. Patricia's wedding party would include her other daughters and her best friend, Colleen, someone she had known since she was twenty-five years old. She called Colleen on the phone and asked her if she was interested in being in the bridal party.

"I'd be happy to," Colleen replied. "What is new in your life?" she asked Patricia.

"Oh, I'm not sure if you heard or not, but John died of a heart attack about eight years ago," Patricia told her friend.

"I'm sorry to hear that," Colleen answered.

"I'm planning a June wedding—June 27, to be exact," Patricia said. "What is new with you?" Patricia asked Colleen.

"I have four children, three girls and one boy. My husband, Paul, and I got a divorce three years ago, and I'm currently dating a wonderful man, Mike, whom I've known for about a year now. I'm not sure, but I think he's about to pop the question," Colleen told Patricia.

"I'm very happy for you. Everyone needs someone," Patricia said.

"Yes, I have to agree with you. Would you like to get together and have lunch sometime?" Colleen asked.

"Yeah, that sounds like a plan to me," Patricia replied.

"How about this Saturday?" Colleen asked.

"Sounds good," Patricia told Colleen.

"Saturday it is then," Colleen said.

"I guess I'll see you Saturday, then," Patricia said.

"Yeah, I'll come over to your place around ten o'clock, so we'll be able to spend the day together," Colleen said to Patricia.

"I'd better let you go and get on with your day," Patricia told her friend.

"Yeah, I have to go to the office," Colleen told Patricia. At that, the two women said their good-byes.

Easter was fast approaching, and Page was busy with the Western Shop. The new spring line was coming in. Page and the girls all loved the spring colors. There were dresses, pants, shirts, shoes, jewelry, and purses. People's orders came in daily. Page had a special order for items that she usually didn't have.

When Saturday arrived, Colleen was at Patricia's house. The two women went to the restaurant.

"This is great—to be together finally and to be catching up on things that have happened in our lives," Patricia said.

The two women enjoyed one another's company; their time together flew by.

"We'll have to get together again soon," the two women agreed.

"Maybe the next time we could go shopping," Colleen suggested.

"Yeah, that sounds good to me," Patricia replied.

At the end of the day, the two women said their good-byes. *Today was well spent,* Patricia thought as she climbed into bed that night.

Chapter 35

A week before Easter, Page suggested to Patricia that they go out to eat. The entire family agreed, so Page made a reservation for all of them at the Longhorn Grill.

Easter arrived before they knew it; the women and men dressed up in their finest Easter attire. The children looked nice as well. The girls all had on colorful dresses, and the boys wore suits and ties. When they got to the restaurant, the hostess led them to their seats. Once they were seated, the waitress asked them what they wanted to drink, and they all helped themselves to the rather huge salad bar.

The women and girls all talked to one another. They seemed at ease as they talked, ate, and had an excellent time together. The women laughed at one another's jokes, and the men seemed to be having a good time as well. Patricia told Page that her idea to have dinner at a restaurant this Easter was very good, and the rest of the family agreed.

After they agreed that they were all finished eating, Timothy suggested that they go see a movie. They picked out a family-oriented movie that they all enjoyed. Seeing the movie after dinner wrapped up their day nicely. It was ten o'clock when they left the theater, and it was one o'clock in the morning when Page climbed into bed.

The next day, Patricia called Page to see what was next. She told Page that Timothy's ideas were unpredictable, and at that, Page said, "Yeah, they certainly are, Mom. His idea to see a movie was a good idea. That must be why you love him so much."

"Yeah, he buys me things out of the blue all the time," Patricia said.

"That's the kind of man to fall in love with," Page told Patricia. "He must really love you!"

"Yeah, in a lot of ways, he is like your dad," Patricia said.

"That's a good thing, because Dad was a very good father, and we kids knew he loved you dearly. Dad always kept things interesting, I'm happy about Timothy being one of the family," Page told her mom and meant it. "I have a doctor's appointment today. I can't wait to have this baby and get my figure back. I feel huge right now, and I'm glad he'll be born in the month of May so I'm able to enjoy your wedding day, Mom."

"Well, I'd better let you go and get on with the rest of your day," Patricia told Page.

"Thanks for calling, Mom, and keep in touch," Page replied.

When at the doctor's office, the doctor said that everything looked good, and he told Page that it looked as if she had a little bit less than a month to go. The baby was due on May 22.

Page went to the Western Shop on a daily basis. Sales were somewhat down as the Easter season was ending, and it seemed that the only things that were selling were on the Easter clearance racks of clothes. The new summer line would be coming in soon and hopefully would boost sales again within a few weeks, Page thought. Page had to cut some of the girls' hours as a result of slow business. She hated to do that to them because they were good, reliable workers. Page kept a few of her most constant employees working forty hours per week, so even their hours were cut until business picked up.

In the middle of May, new shipments were coming in. Page increased some of the girls' hours. Women seemed to be out shopping more as the weather was improving; they had cabin fever.

Page awoke a few hours after she went to bed one night in May, and she was indeed in labor. She phoned her mom in order to ask her to watch the kids, and then she called 911. The ambulance was at the house within the hour. They took her to the emergency room, where she was in labor for about three hours.

The baby was emerging, so the doctor told her to bear down and push.

The baby came quickly this time.

"It is a boy, as expected," Dr. Gordon told Page.

Page was happy about her new baby boy but sad at the same time, as Blake would never know his son, and her son would never know his dad. *Life goes on, regardless,* Page thought to herself. "I'm not yet sure what to name him," Page said. Page took him in her arms and told him, "It's just you and I, and your brothers and sisters, little one." Page chose to breastfeed.

Three days after the baby was born, Page decided to name him Blake Samuel Turner. Page liked calling him Blake after his dad. At least she could carry on Blake's name, if nothing else.

On the fourth day, Dr. Gordon sent Page and Blake home. Patricia picked the two of them up, and Blake's sisters and brothers sat in the backseat. Taylor was five years old now and would be turning six, the twins were three years old, Faith was a year old, and then there was Blake. Page thought to herself, *It's just me and the kids.*

Once at home, Page and the kids settled in, and Taylor got to hold her baby brother. It made her feel like a big girl. Page was back to running the Western Shop within a month. She was one woman you just couldn't hold down.

The wedding was right around the corner—two days away—so the wedding party practiced for the big day.

The day of the wedding, Patricia had butterflies in her stomach. The usual wedding rituals were performed. They placed rings on one another's fingers, and the bride and groom kissed. Afterward, they were introduced as the new Mr. and Mrs. Timothy Lambert. The wedding reception lasted well into the night with eating, dancing, drinking, talking, and laughing, all the people having a good time. That night, Patricia and Timothy got a motel room, and the next day, they were on the airplane headed to Disney World for a two-week honeymoon.

Page went home to an empty house, got the kids all into bed, and then climbed into bed herself. As she fell asleep, her mind drifted back to Blake and the tragic accident, and at that, she cried herself to sleep.

Chapter 36

Baby Blake got up and was crying at five o'clock in the morning. He was bottle-fed now. Page changed him, fed him, and went right back to sleep until eight o'clock. He was an excellent baby; he seldom fussed unless he was hungry or he needed his diaper changed.

Summer came and went rapidly, as it usually does. Taylor would be in kindergarten now. It was a big day for her, as it was her first day of school. She seemed happy and a little unsure of what to expect. Page tried to reassure her that she would do just fine and everything would be all right. Page hugged her before she boarded the bus.

Newlyweds Patricia and Timothy had a wonderful time on her honeymoon. They both came back relaxed, tanned, and happy.

Page's phone rang around ten o'clock in the morning, and when Page answered it, she heard Patricia asking her how she and her grandchildren were doing. "Everyone here is good, Mom. Taylor went to school today. It was her first day," Page told her mom.

"Oh, I'm glad. How did she do?" Patricia asked.

"She did really good for her first day. She was unsure about what to expect, and she was excited and a little bit scared at the same time," Page told her mom.

"That is understandable," Patricia said.

"Well, I have to go and feed Blake—he's crying—and I need to make breakfast for the other children as well," Page told Patricia. "How was your honeymoon?" Page asked.

"We had a good time, but it was over too soon," Patricia said.

"Yeah, good times go by quickly, Mom," Page said.

"Unfortunately, they do seem to."

The two women said their good-byes and got on with the rest of their day.

Page fed the kids their breakfast as she got ready to go to the Western Shop. The new fall line would soon be in; its colors screamed fall and made one think of the holidays to come. The girls' hours were increasing again, and business was good.

It had been almost a year since Blake's death. Page missed being in a man's arms, and she was searching for someone to be in her life again— someone she could confide in.

The Thanksgiving season was near. Page, Patricia, and the other girls all decided to chip in and make the meal together this year. That would take the brunt off a single person doing everything.

One morning, Page got up to take care of Blake. He was fussing because he was cutting teeth, and Page tried to comfort him. Page went to work early that day since she was up already. That day, around noon, an attractive guy came in and asked for Page's advice about a jacket he liked; he wanted to make a special order. He ordered a pair of cowboy boots and a black leather fringed jacket. Page didn't tell him, but she liked him, and when he ordered his stuff, she learned that his name was Luke Timberlake. She wanted to tell him that she was attracted to him; she didn't realize that he also liked her. After she met him, she noticed that he had become a regular at the Western Shop.

"Would you like to go out to dinner some night after work?" Luke finally asked Page.

"Yes, I would love to. I thought you would never ask," Page said.

"How about Friday night?" Luke asked.

"Sounds good to me," Page said.

Friday night came, and Page was ready when Luke arrived. She wore a pair of her favorite jeans, a red sweater, and knee-high boots. She was lovely in his eyes. He was dressed nicely as well. He had on jeans, a blue shirt, and a denim jacket.

They went to the Steakhouse Grill. Once there, they ordered what they wanted to eat. They both decided to order a rack of ribs, salad, and beer.

"Tell me about yourself," Luke said. He was instantly attracted to her.

"Well, I have five kids by the same man, three girls and two boys. Taylor is six, the twins are three, Faith is two, and Blake is six months. My husband died one night when we were on the way to our beach house. It was raining hard. He couldn't see. The car spun out of control, and there was a tractor-trailer truck coming in the opposite direction. He hit the driver's side head-on, and Blake died on impact."

"The same thing happened to me," Luke said. "My wife, Paula, died of brain cancer instantly. We have two kids together, Rebecca and Doug.

Rebecca is five, and Doug is three. I loved her dearly. It was a very unfortunate thing."

"Yes, I agree with you," Page said. "Blake's death was unfortunate also, and I loved him dearly. Blake had an affair at our beach house with a woman named Laura, and he had a boy with her because of it. His name is Shawn. He is about three years old now. I loved Blake enough that I forgave him. I was working all the time, getting the Western Shop going, and when I wasn't doing that, I was spending time with my kids. I was going to make up lost time with Blake when I found the note to Blake from Laura," Page said. "It almost cost us our marriage."

"That shows you are very forgiving and caring," Luke told Page.

"It makes you wonder why things turn out the way they do," Page said.

"A lot of things go wrong in life, but you really have to try to make the best of things," Luke said. After several hours at the bar, they started getting tipsy. "I think I'm falling in love with you, Page."

"Yeah, same here," Page said.

"What do you say we get a motel room?" Luke asked.

"Sounds good to me," Page said.

Once in the room, Luke and Page started kissing and hugging. One thing led to another, and they started to undress each other. Luke said, "You are the most beautiful woman I've seen. I want you badly." "Yes, and I want you as well," Page told Luke.

Before they knew it, they were making out on the sofa. Then they ended up in bed. Page woke up the next morning in Luke's arms, and at that, they had sex once more, and then again in the shower. Afterward, they got dressed and went to a nearby restaurant for breakfast. They had pancakes, sausage, oatmeal, orange juice, and coffee.

"I absolutely loved being with you," Page remarked as he took her back to her place.

"Yeah, I feel the same way," Luke replied. "How about we go to a movie and then dinner afterward tonight?" Luke suggested.

"You are very unpredictable and exciting to be with—those are two traits I'm in love with about you already, Luke Timberlake."

It was nearly eleven o'clock when Luke dropped Page off at her house. "I'll pick you up around five o'clock tonight," Luke said.

Luke and Page embraced and kissed each other long and hard, and then Page walked up the steps to her house. That day, Page felt young again; there was something about a hot, new romantic relationship that made her feel this way. Page was just about to step into the shower when she heard the phone ring. When she answered, she heard a woman's voice, and Page guessed that it was Laura.

"Is Blake there?" the woman asked.

"I'm afraid he isn't. He was in an awful accident about a year ago, and when he got hit, he died instantly. A big tractor-trailer truck hit him. It was raining, and neither Blake nor the other driver could see what was in front of them," Page said. "I was in the passenger seat, and I had a pretty bad concussion, but somehow, I survived."

"Oh, that sounds absolutely awful," Laura said with a shocked tone of voice.

"Is this Laura?" Page asked.

"Yes, it is," Laura replied.

"Well, I guess there is very little to say after that," Laura told Page.

At that, Page showered and got dressed. She put on a pretty blue dress and a pair of high-heeled, blue leather shoes, and she wore a blue bow in her hair. She looked very pretty. When Luke arrived, he also commented on how good she looked. He looked good also, wearing a tan leather blazer, tan-colored slacks, a yellow shirt, and brown leather cowboy boots. The two of them held hands as they walked to the movie theater. While there, they had popcorn and saw a movie that they both enjoyed. After the movie, they talked about the film and walked to a nearby restaurant. They both picked out a fish dinner and wine to drink. "The fish here is very good," Page remarked.

"Yeah, fish is one of my favorite foods," Luke said.

The two of them talked about their kids, their jobs, and how much they loved one another. "You never told me what you do for a living," Page said.

"I'm a loan officer at the National Bank. I own 250 acres," Luke said. "It's a good-sized ranch, and I have thirty horses. I have a ranch hand who takes care of the horses. I make a lot of my money off the ranch, when we have shows and such."

That's funny, because that is what Blake did for his living. He was a ranch hand at my mother's ranch," Page told Luke.

"That is very amusing." Luke laughed as he said it. "You must love horses as much as I do!" he exclaimed.

"I do love horses," Page remarked.

"That's good. We seem to have a lot in common," Luke replied. "I'm afraid that I'm falling in love with you faster than I expected to, Page. Let's plan on a trip to Paris after Christmas is over. I took Paula there on our honeymoon, and she absolutely loved it there!" Luke suggested to Page with much excitement in his voice.

"Everything about you sounds amazing, Luke. Blake and I went there several times, and I loved it as well."

"I made the right decision, falling head over heels in love with you," the two of them agreed and laughed as they did so.

After the two of them left the restaurant, they spent another night at the motel, and as they went to sleep that night, they both thought that they had made the right choice in partners.

How could life happen much the same way for two completely different couples?

Chapter 37

When they awoke the next morning, they indulged in their lovemaking first thing and again in the shower. As they got dressed, Luke teased that he would like to have her again and again, because he couldn't get enough of her. "I love you, Page. I never expected things to go this way or this rapidly, although I'm happy they are."

Page thought that Luke and Blake were a lot alike, and she was very happy that she had the chance to find true love twice in the same lifetime.

Luke and Page went to the same little restaurant as they had the day before. Once there, they each ordered eggs, bacon, toast, and coffee. Page also ordered orange juice, and they both had water. They talked and talked, and as they did, all the people around them could sense that they were in love.

"I forgot to tell you something, Page. I inherited my ranch from my dad. My mom died when I was only eight years old. My dad is in an old-age home and has been since last spring."

"Oh, I'm sorry to hear that," Page said. "My dad died instantly from a heart attack. He was fifty-six years old, and he never knew any of my children. In fact, I had just discovered that I was expecting Taylor when he passed."

"Wow, it really does seem that we've both been through a lot of losses," Luke said.

"Yeah, maybe fate brought us together," Page told Luke.

"It almost seems that it did," Luke remarked.

As they left the restaurant, Luke suggested that they take a walk in the park. They held hands and chatted back and forth, at ease.

Afterward, they walked back to Page's house, and they no more than stepped into the house when they started undressing each other. After that, they got into bed, explored each other, and had a good time together.

After making love several times, Page made them each a chicken salad, and they had wine at the bar set up in Page's house, which had been Blake's idea.

"You know, I have a bar in my house as well." Luke laughed as he said it.

"Words can't describe how I'm feeling," Page told Luke and meant it.

"We were both alone with no one in our lives until fate stepped in and brought us together. I'm so thankful for the Western Shop," Luke said.

"Yeah, so am I," Page replied. "If it wasn't for the shop, we would never have met. Well, there is a saying that things happen for the best."

"Yeah, I've heard that saying also," Luke said.

"If things happen for the best, then why do so many bad things happen?" Page asked.

"I don't know. It's God's will," Luke replied. It was midnight as Luke left Page's house. "I love you, and I'll miss you," Luke told Page.

"Yeah, same here," Page said.

"I'll call you this week every time I get the chance. Next weekend, plan on going out somewhere together," Luke told her.

That night, as Page climbed into bed, she thought that she was truly in love with Luke, and she knew how lucky she was.

Chapter 38

Page got up the next morning and made breakfast for the kids. Then she took a shower and got dressed. When the babysitter got to the house, Page went to the Western Shop the way she always did, and when she got there, it was busy, as it was soon to be Christmas. They had orders of all kinds coming in, and sales were up.

"I like this time of year," Page said. "It brings in extra business."

That night, when Page got home, Patricia called to see what was new, as she hadn't heard from Page for quite some time.

"Hi, Page," Patricia said. "What is new with you?"

"Oh, I met someone. His name is Luke Timberlake. He came into the shop and ordered a couple things."

"Oh, that is wonderful! You need another man in your life," Patricia said.

"He is a lot like Blake, and Mom, he has already asked me to go to Paris with him. He was alone and lonely too. His wife passed away of brain cancer at an early age. She died instantly, just like Blake did."

"That is unfortunate for Luke, and I'm very sorry to hear that. He sounds like a good guy, though," Patricia said.

"Yeah, he is, and it is showing already. How could I be so lucky? He owns 250 acres. He inherited the land from his dad. His mom passed away when he was eight years old."

"I'm sorry to hear that, but I'm very impressed by the amount of acreage he owns. What do you say we do our usual Christmas shopping?" Patricia asked.

"That sounds good to me, Mom."

LIFE'S TWISTS

So the two women agreed to go the following Saturday.

"Luke and I are going to do something special this coming weekend," Page told her mom. "He is spontaneous; that is one of his better traits," Page said.

"You and I have good men in our lives," both women agreed.

"Well, Mom, I have to make the kids' supper, and I want to relax a little while before bedtime, so I'll talk to you later."

When Page awoke the next day, she did the usual things. She made breakfast, took a shower, got dressed, and went to the Western Shop, almost like clockwork. There were only two weeks until Christmas, although it was difficult to believe another year was almost over. The usual things were going on at the store that day. The store was extremely busy and fast paced, and that night, when Page got home, she had just jumped into the shower when Luke called.

"Hi, babe," Luke exclaimed. "I'm sorry I haven't called you, but it has been extremely busy at the bank the past two days."

"Speaking of busy, it has been absolutely crazy at the store, and your order came in today also. I was going to call you around two o'clock, but I didn't get a chance to."

"Do you want to go to Vegas this weekend? We could leave on Thursday so we would have a couple of extra days."

"Yeah, I would absolutely love to!" Page exclaimed.

"Then Vegas it is! I'll pick you up around nine o'clock in the morning," Luke replied.

"You certainly are unpredictable, Luke Timberlake, and I love you more than words can describe."

"Yes, and I love you as much," Luke told Page. "Well, I'd better let you go, as I know you have to spend time with your kids. I'll see you around nine Thursday morning. I love you, and take care," Luke told Page.

After getting off the phone with Luke, Page could hardly believe how lucky she was to have met such a wonderful man.

Thursday came quickly; Page had packed the night before. In the morning, she took a shower early. She was picking out what she would wear that day when Luke showed up at the door.

"Hello," Page said when she answered the door.

Luke took her in his arms and told her how much he loved her and had missed her.

"Yes, I missed you as much," Page said.

Luke and Page made love in the shower and then got dressed.

On the way, they stopped as needed, and once in Las Vegas, they picked out a restaurant they both thought they would like. They talked at ease with each other, as they usually did. The restaurant had a rather huge food bar, which was excellently set up, and after they were finished, they stopped at a bar and had a few drinks. Luke had beer, and Page indulged in mixed drinks. Afterward, back at the hotel suite, they had sex over and over again. "I love you so much, and I can't seem to get enough of you," Luke told Page.

They talked until they fell asleep.

The time they spent together in Vegas went by quickly, and soon, it was time to go home and get back to the usual things—work, family, life, etc. Only five days remained until Christmas, which came fast, and the family went to Patricia's house, as planned. Page introduced Luke to her siblings, and they all seemed to like him; he fit in well as he talked to them with ease.

After the Christmas season was over, Luke and Page flew to Paris, as Luke promised they would. On New Year's Eve, Luke proposed to Page.

"Will you marry me, Page?" he asked.

"I would be happy to," Page replied.

While there, they had an excellent time together, and the last night they spent there, Page had a feeling that she would have Luke's child. She didn't know why; it was just her intuition, and she thought that, while life has its twists, it is what you do with your life that counts the most.

www.ingramcontent.com/pod-product-compliance
Lightning Source LLC
LaVergne TN
LVHW040155080526
838202LV00042B/3163